THE
GODS
OF
GREYFALL
COLLECTION

A.J. NORRIS

Cover Designed by: Deranged Doctor Design
Edited by: Felicia A. Sullivan
Formatted by: A.J. Norris

Author's Note: A version of part one of this collection was previously published in the limited-edition anthology, Haunted by Love.

ISBN: 978-1-7320238-1-9

First Edition: April 2018

DEDICATION

For my readers

PART ONE

NIGHT GODS

CHAPTER ONE

DRU

Dru perched atop a stone gargoyle on the tallest building in Greyfall, scanning, listening to the city below. He was high enough that if someone looked up they wouldn't be able to tell him apart from the statue he sat on. Still, he could hear the traffic noises far below. Discerning the sounds came easily to him with his differentiating hearing.

Born in a government funded lab twenty-six years before, Dru carried the DNA of a human, a demon, and the ancient Egyptian god Osiris, and was raised as a soldier. He fished a one-shot vial out of his leather jacket pocket and tipped it back. The blood slid down the back of his throat. Red wasn't a necessity of life for him, but the source of his powers—rapid healing, acute senses, and night vision. And his most favorite, vaporizing, or vaping, as he and his fellow Bator called it. He tossed the tiny glass cylinder over his shoulder and it landed in the growing pile of shards outside the roof access door.

Voices of a nearby demon Collective slowly rose. Ordinary humans couldn't hear the sounds, only others with demon blood in their veins could. Dru pitched his head forward and listened. The demons of the Collective attacked cars on the expressway that ran across the north end of the city. The stretch of road where they gathered was inside his patrol territory. Good. He was in the mood for dismembering someone tonight.

Like most nights since she had said goodbye, he couldn't get the last words she said to him out of his mind.

I hate you.

Kalani had been in the Bator Patrol Guard Training Program with him. Ten years ago she chose to leave, separating them. She had wanted him drop out too. Choose her over a life of servitude that he neither disliked nor begrudged. And to do what, blend into human society? Leave the one place he was accepted, where he didn't have to hide his eyes? She was asking him to leave his entire family behind. He couldn't do it.

Another one of Dru's talents was the ability to hone in on one individual and see through their eyes. He closed his and brought forth the images that came to him in flashes. A red SUV traveling west. Four passengers, two women and two men. He could only get a glimpse of one woman's face and the back of the other's head. They all screamed though. Dru backed out of the demon's mind and took a swan dive off the skyscraper. The wind blew his hair behind him. With a thought, his corporeal form began turning to a fine black mist. Starting at his feet, a vapor swirled around, engulfing and swallowing him until he was gone, leaving behind wisps of dark mist that dissipated within seconds.

* * *

Kalani

Kalani stretched her legs out in the back seat of her friend Benny's SUV. Jade glanced over at her from the seat beside her and smiled. Her best friend looked nervous. She was a bit shy, and this was a first date for her and Benny. However, neither was aware Kalani was setting them up.

"So glad you came with tonight," Jade said.

"Yeah, thank God you called, she's been a hermit," Rob, Kalani's boyfriend, said from the front passenger seat.

Kalani smiled. "I'm not a hermit. I work from home so I don't see a reason to leave the house."

"I call that a hermit," Benny said.

"I'm a recluse, there's a difference." Kalani had left the house, she had gone grocery shopping.

Greyfall's demon Collective had been active tonight. Her senses weren't as strong as they used to be. Every year she refused to drink Red, the fainter the connection became. Now, unless there was a large gathering or activity near her, she couldn't hear them moving about the area. And she still had to focus her concentration. This lack of knowledge of their whereabouts left her edgy. However, the more demons, the easier it was to hear them.

A buzzing in the back of her mind made her turn around. She batted the air. Demon activity was nearby. Benny took the on ramp to the expressway. Not the place humans should be. Ever. But people had to get from one place to another. She exhaled a shaky breath and asked, "Why are we taking the highway?"

"It's the fastest route," Benny said.

And made them easy targets for demons.

"Relax. There haven't been any attacks in months."

"That doesn't mean anything."

"The Bator will—"

"Bator can't defend against everything."

Rob glanced over his shoulder at her. "We'll only be on this road for a few minutes."

"A few too lon—"

Something heavy hit the rear windshield. Kalani ducked. Jade yelped. "You were saying?" Another large object smashed the glass, shattering it. Jade screamed again. Benny slowed the car.

"Don't slow down!" Kalani shouted, but it was too late.

CHAPTER TWO

DRU

Dru reappeared in the same manner as he had disappeared, in a whirling cloud of vapor. He landed on the hood of the red SUV. Screams pierced the air. He didn't get nervous anymore going up against a group of demons. This was just part of his everyday routine. And this carload of screaming, terrified humans was nothing more than ordinary. One demon held onto the hood while pounding his fist into the windshield. In another few punches, he'd be through the glass. Dru grabbed his waist from behind and flung him onto the gravel shoulder. The driver slammed on the brakes.

"Don't slow down!" Dru yelled. He had anticipated the panicked response and vaped onto the roof. Two demons tore at the metal, pulling the steel off in strips. He kicked one in the chin, flipping him ass over feet. He landed on the pavement with a bounce. The other yanked his feet out from under him and Dru went down on his back, his head slamming onto the unforgiving windshield. The demon grabbed the sides of his hooded jacket by the lapels then drove a fist into his cheek. Dru had never seen this young demon before who was evidently unschooled about Bator strength. Dru grinned at the weak punch as he brought his head back around. The demon caught his gaze and stared for a second. They had the same slit-pupiled eyes, only Dru's irises were reddish-orange and full-blooded demons' were deep purple. Maybe he had never seen a Bator up close before? Dru backhanded the ignorant twerp. "Get off me!" he shouted, shoving him off the roof.

The car pulled to the side of the road. "Don't stop!" Man, why did they never listen? It was much easier flinging the dastards from a moving car and fewer were likely to join the attack. They couldn't vape, but they could run fast, and three sped toward them. "Go!" The car stayed parked idling on the shoulder. *"Drive!"*

Dru's knees hit the roof as the SUV rocked from side to side. There was a muffled scream. Somehow a demon had gotten inside. Another scream rose from the hole in the top of the car. He peered into the SUV. It hissed and its beady eyes glowed in the darkened interior.

The demon sat wedged between two women with his arm around the neck of the one with dark hair. "You come any closer, I snap her neck," he growled.

"You'd do that? How would your Collective feel about that? Tell you what, you go ahead and do it." Dru met the woman's eyes. The color of them didn't suit her at all and they looked fake as hell. He didn't acknowledge her sneer. Of all the cars on the highway, these demons had picked this one? What were the chances?

"I swear it!"

"Do it then!" Dru snapped.

The eyes of the woman in the chokehold widened and the other one screamed. The front passenger grappled for the door handle. How far did he think he would get on foot with a demon chasing him?

"Wha-what, no!" the man behind the wheel shrieked.

"Drive or die. Your choice," Dru spat toward him.

"There's a demon in the car."

"No shit, and there's three behind us. Take your pick."

* * *

Kalani

Before she even caught a glimpse of Dru, she'd smelled him. She hated him as much now as she did ten years ago. His scent made it worse. Why did he have to smell so damn good?

Bastard.

She really hated him. He ignored the curled-lipped look she gave him, further irritating her.

Jade plastered herself to the door. Kalani's best friend's voice grew hoarse with all the screaming. She gripped the door handle.

"Stay in the car," Kalani wheezed. She wanted to tell Jade it was safer inside the car.

"What's it going to be, driver?" Dru asked Benny.

The car lurched forward.

Thank God.

Except the door next to Jade flung open and she leapt out.

"No!" Kalani's yell had been much louder in her own head than what came out.

"Go! Go!" Dru barked. He vaped inside the car, taking Jade's vacant seat. In all of a couple of milliseconds he unsheathed a 9" dagger holstered to his chest and yanked the demon by the hair, exposing his neck. Kalani closed her eyes and mouth, turning her head. Stinky demon blood in her mouth was something she wanted to avoid. Dru ripped the blade across the demon's throat. The act happened so swiftly that one second the back of the driver's seat was black and the next it was covered in purple phosphorescent demon blood.

The demon crumpled to the floorboards, already in the process of rapid decay. Soon it would be ash and flake away. Jade screamed. The vehicle jerked from side to side as Benny merged onto the road. Kalani twisted and looked out the back window as the vehicle sped away.

On the gravel shoulder, two demons held Jade by the arms and legs. Kalani willed her friend to keep fighting, as if she could hear her. Somehow she must have, because she writhed and bucked. Where was the third—?

BOOM!

The roof depressed where the demon landed. "Better deal with that," she said to Dru. He disappeared in a swirl of black vapor.

Something heavy, a body perhaps, banged onto the roof a moment later.

"Oh shiiit!" the voice that hollered didn't belong to Dru. Despite her negative feelings toward him, she was relieved.

He poked his head through the hole in the roof. "Everyone all right in here?"

Benny and Rob nodded their heads like idiots.

"No. They took Jade!" Kalani said.

"Are you hurt?"

"They took Jade!"

"I know."

"Aren't you going to go after her?" she narrowed her eyes at him, seething.

Dru stared back with cold eyes. "Be my guest."

"Benny, turn the car around."

"I wouldn't do that if I were you," Dru warned. "I also suggest you get to where you are going quickly." He vaped inside the SUV. "I'll ride with you until you get off the freeway."

"Will they be b-back?" Rob stammered.

"No," Kalani said. "They got what they wanted." She knew the demons wouldn't want her even when one of them had his arm wrapped around her neck. He'd scented her immediately after slipping himself in through the shattered back window. He'd grabbed her by mistake, not knowing which one of them was Bator. A tear ran down her face.

"Crying won't help," Dru said. The statement may have sounded callous to Benny and Rob, but Kalani knew he hadn't meant it that way. He was being truthful. Blunt.

She swiped a finger under each eye and sniffed. "I'm not."

He sat mutely, wiping both sides of his dagger's blade off on his leather pant leg.

Kalani huffed. "Whatever."

"Did I say anything?"

"You didn't have to. Your silence says a lot."

Dru looked at her sideways. "What are you talking about? You don't know what I'm thinking. You don't even know me."

"Yes, I do. Don't you recognize me?"

He shook his head.

She gasped. "You. Ooooh. I hate you."

"Calm dow—"

"Do you two know each other?" Benny asked, glancing in the rearview mirror. Rob craned his head in her direction.

"No," Dru said at the same time she said, "Yes."

Fury shook within Kalani. "Get out of this car!"

"Not until you get off this road."

"Benny, take the next exit so we can lose this asshole." She stared out the window.

"Asshole? Why am I an asshole?"

"Yes, asshole, that's what I said. And you know *why*."

"I'm out. Good luck to you three."

"Yeah, there should be four, not three. Asshole."

"What was I supposed to do, go after her and leave you three with two demons? Odds you survived would be zilch. Protocol states—"

"I don't care about your stupid rules."

Dru took a deep breath. "Sorry about your friend, but not I'm sorry I saved the three of you instead of only one of you."

"There's still time, you could go after her."

"No. Even if I could, I'm not going to march into the Collective realm and demand they return one human. Like that's going to happen. Are you crazy?"

He was right. Dammit. She'd do it herself, if she hadn't stopped taking blood years ago. A Bator's demon DNA allowed them to enter the demon realm, which was a pocket of space in another dimension. Human women were forcibly taken and used by the demons for their blood. They were never seen again. Mostly. On occasion, one would escape. However, these women became catatonic shortly after making it back to Earth. It was a medical mystery which baffled scientists around the world.

"See, this is why I couldn't do what you do anymore," Kalani said.

"We have protocols in place for a reason. It's too

dangerous. Can't afford to lose—forget it, you never understood."

Rob mouthed, *What?* Kalani didn't react to him, although she met his eyes.

"That's right," she said. "You people think one life doesn't matter, but it does."

"Not when three more are at stake. You think they wouldn't kill all of you? It's a damn sport to them."

Kalani took a deep breath through her nose. "You could've gone after her."

"No, I couldn't. There were too many."

"You had no problem throwing them off the car."

"Easier while it's moving, you know that."

Confusion crossed Rob's face.

"I gotta go. My shift is over." Dru holstered his dagger and vaped from the backseat.

"How do you know that Bator?" Rob asked. Humans knew about Bator and the role they played in the protection of the human species. Demons didn't want to take over the world, they only desired the blood of women, much like a fly was attracted to shit. They couldn't help it; the scent of Red intoxicated them. Luckily for the humans, Bator had been created to fight demons and with a little blood they had powers not unlike vampires. Although vampires didn't exist according to scientists, descendants of Osiris did.

"I've seen him before."

"Sounded like more than that."

"It's not." Kalani put her face in her hands. Was he seriously getting jealous right now? Did anyone but her care about Jade? "I hate him," she muttered.

"To hate him, don't you have to know him?" Benny interjected.

Not helping, Benny.

She rubbed her eyes, forgetting about her contacts that concealed her slit-pupils. Kalani blinked a couple of times before they righted themselves. Rob didn't know she was Bator. They hadn't been dating long enough for her to feel comfortable revealing that tiny detail to him. It totally wasn't fair, she knew this. "Can we just get off this road?"

Benny took the next exit. Demons tended to stick to the freeways because like Dru had said, it was sport for them. They enjoyed the hunt. Even though they only captured women, anyone who got in their way died.

Oh, Jade...

"How do you know the Bator? You never answered my question."

"I don't know him, didn't you hear him?"

"He talked like you were familiar with their protocols. Why would he say—"

"Pull over and let me out," Kalani said.

"That's not a good idea," Benny said.

Kalani held her breath. She couldn't have any conversation right now that kept her trapped in this car. Jade needed her. "Pull over at the next bus stop."

"You're not getting out of this car," Rob told her.

"Why not?" she snarled.

"It's not saf—"

"We're off the freeway. Benny, pull over," she demanded.

"No! If you pull over Benny, man, I swear," Rob warned.

"You swear?" Kalani glared at Benny in the rearview mirror. "Stop this car now."

Benny turned into the gas station they were about to pass.

"What are you doing?" Rob barked at Benny.

Kalani seethed. Dru's presence niggled at the back of her neck, sending tingles down her spine. The male wasn't getting under her skin, but tunneling beneath it with sharp sticks. They had been inseparable during her time in the training program. Dru had entertained leaving the Patrol Guard for a better life, one without serving others for nothing in return except a pitiful salary and ridiculously teensy apartment in a building downtown that resembled a prison. Kalani thought he truly wanted to leave. Yet when the time came to decide, he'd backed out. She hated his choice. Still did. The SUV stopped. She pulled the door handle but it was locked. "Unlock the door."

"It's not safe," Benny said evenly.

"I'll be fine."

"How? Those demons probably tracked us here," Rob said.

Kalani took a deep breath, sensing nothing but humans around and the demon who she knew owned this gas station. He was one of the good ones, though. The guy wore contact lens too and hated dirt like all demons. She herself got seriously annoyed with dirt on her shoes or hands. However, full-blooded demons tended to do more than despise it, they possessed some type of phobia. "They didn't."

"How do you know? You got demon radar or some shit?" Rob's exasperated tone irritated her. Demons didn't abduct Bator unless they had a good reason. They considered their blood inferior to human. Funny, she considered their blood nasty, so...

"Maybe. They came out with it last year. Didn't you know?"

Benny made an amused sound. Rob rolled his eyes. "You're funny."

"I wasn't trying to be."

Rob crossed his arms. "Who was the Bator who helped us?"

"Don't you even care about what happened

to Jade?" A fresh prickling wave washed over her body. The kind of sensation that made you woozy. She gasped.

"Nice try. Don't change the subject."

"What's the matter, you jealous?" All right, that wasn't the best thing to say. Rob was liable to mistake it for an admission.

"So you admit it, you do know him?"

And there it is.

"Don't be ridiculous. How would I know him? Humans and Bator don't exactly mix it up on a regular basis." They didn't, most feared Bator. "Unlock the door, Benny."

Benny raised his hands next to his head. "I agree with Rob, you shouldn't get out of the car."

"I want to go home."

"I'll take you."

"No thank you."

"What's his name?" Rob asked. "And how long have you been fucking him?"

Kalani's chest vibrated, as if her insides had decided to grind together like the inner workings of an engine seizing. Rob hadn't seemed the controlling, suspicious type. She thanked God for not having slept with him yet. "I have not *fucked* Dru!" That was no lie. They had been sixteen when she had known him. Except shit!

Rob snorted with derision. "I *knew* you knew him."

"Screw. You." Kalani's fangs descended, causing her lips to part.

"No thank—"

Anger broke through her ability to suppress growling. A deep rumble came out of her mouth. The inhuman sound surprised all three of them. Her lips peeled back off her fangs. Benny's face lost all the color and Rob ducked away from her.

"Unlock the door," Kalani roared, pitching her head forward.

"Holy shit! She's a demon!" Benny screamed. Rob just screamed.

"Let me out before I rip this door off." They probably imagined she had said, "I'll rip your head off."

"D-don't kill us." Benny hit buttons next to him until he found the "Unlock."

Once she heard the double click, Kalani yanked the door handle, escaping outside. "I'm Bator, assholes!" Demons didn't have fangs. What idiots.

The last thing Rob said as she slammed the door shut was, "Glad I didn't sleep with her."

CHAPTER THREE

KALANI

Rain started falling the second Benny's SUV pulled out of the gas station parking lot. Kalani would never see either of them again. Rob, she was okay with, but Benny... She exhaled slowly. He and Jade were her best friends.

There weren't any demons around that she

sensed. Within a few minutes, the rain plastered her hair to her scalp and drenched her clothes.

She walked along on the sidewalk toward the bus stop. Ten years ago, she'd stopped taking Red and asked to leave the Bator training program. Lab-born hybrids like herself and Dru could leave the program after their sixteenth year. They weren't forced to continue.

Anyone that stayed was given a ridiculously small salary for living expenses. Because of this, many Bator lived at the Patrol Guard headquarters for free. She had wanted more from life and believed Dru had too.

Kalani sat in the bus stop shelter and waited for a bus to take her downtown. She was headed back to the place she despised more than Dru, and never had imagined any scenario where she'd voluntarily return. Jade was worth it though. Kalani had confided in her about what she was and the woman still accepted her.

Bator were freaks, but her best friend never feared Kalani or made her feel like an outsider, even though that was how she herself felt most of the time.

Kalani didn't drink Red but still had the cravings like an addict. Blood reacted differently with a Bator's DNA than a full-blooded demon.

She swiped her bus pass card and sat in the seat

closest to the door. A man sitting across from her had watched her from the moment she got on the bus until she sat down.

"Your eyes are unusual," he said.

She quickly looked at the floor.

"Aw, don't do that, it was a compliment."

"Oh, thanks." The contacts she wore had to be opaque, and consequently, their color looked unnatural. For the first sixteen years of her life, she had only known their natural color, reddish-orange, like mini fires. Great, now she felt self-conscious. She didn't raise her eyes for the duration of the ride.

The Bator building stood five hundred feet and had gargoyles perched on top. She knew not all of what sat up there were statues. Her kind always dreamed they could fly. Kalani smirked, finding the concept so stupid and what was dumber, she dreamed that too. Still. Since as long as she remembered, Kalani had flying dreams.

The drab gray cement building appeared not to have any windows or doors. This wasn't true. The windows were narrow slats, recessed into the outer walls, two feet in, much like a prison. Any entrances looked even less welcoming, if that was possible. A large arch on the front of the building, which was the main door, appeared to be a decoration stuck to the side. In the middle hung the Patrol Guard logo, Osiris' crook and flail. She wouldn't be getting inside through the front door.

The building had secrets—ventilation shafts accessed through a drainage tunnel in the alley next to it. When she'd been a member of the training program, Kalani and her friends had snuck in and out to do normal teenage things. Or at least, what they thought was normal based on the few TV shows they were allowed to watch.

Kalani looked around before slipping into the alley, making sure nobody was paying attention. She heaved the steel grate cover from a drainage tunnel and peered inside. Light from the building next door shone down through the gap in the asphalt. However, the illumination wouldn't travel far.

She lowered herself into the tunnel and dropped down another five feet to the floor. Water splashed around her shoes. The coolness seeped through the canvas of her Chuck Taylors. Thankfully, less than two inches of stinky, metallic smelling water covered the cement floor. She crinkled her nose. Fishing out her cell phone, she turned on the flashlight and shined the light in both directions, only a glance before shutting it off.

Moving swiftly, Kalani counted out the number of paces to the ventilation duct. This one emptied into one of the below ground nurseries. This time of night, most of the staff would have gone home.

She ripped off the vented sheet metal cover. The rivets flew in every direction, plunking into the water and pinging off the rounded wall behind her.

Even though she was almost as strong as a male Bator when at her full potential, she was petite and fit through the shaft. Full potential meant she had her fill of Red.

She sniffed the air. The coppery smell increased. Where was it coming from? Not the water at her feet. The scent grew stronger when she stuck her head into the vent. Dru's face appeared in her mind. Ever since she ran into him, smelled him, her craving for blood had risen. The draw to seek it out had been tolerable before tonight. Her mouth watered, she licked her lips. How could she go back inside this place? She thought of Jade. No, she'd find another way to help her. If the craving for Red was this strong, and she'd heard it increased with age, how could she ever break free again from this life?

She steeled herself, pivoted away from the vent, and ran for the drainage opening, water splashing in her wake.

A warm, prickling sensation traveled up her spine into her mouth. She gasped.

Red...

The hole above her seemed so far away. Kalani crouched, then sprang into the air, reaching with one hand for the edge of the hole. And...missed.

She hadn't even come close.

Damn!

She didn't have the power of a fully satiated, blood filled Bator. Sure, opening a grate and flimsy vent cover took strength, but power leaping was another thing entirely. She attempted the feat again. And failed. The pressure inside her body tripled and her heart thumped so hard she shook. Red oozed down the walls. Her breath caught.

She swiped at the wall and brought the moisture up to her nose, licked. She screamed when she tasted water, not blood. All rational thought left her mind. Red was the only thing remaining.

Acting only on instinct, Kalani sprinted for the vent. She threw herself head-first down the shaft, with her arms stretched out in front.

CHAPTER FOUR

DRU

Covered in demon blood, Dru stepped through the roof access door where he lived with the rest of the Patrol Guard. He couldn't wait to decontaminate in the shower. He'd taken his time coming home. Seeing Kalani had messed him up more than he wanted to admit. Gods, she was beautiful. Her petite body and Bator scent made his mouth water.

Covering up his desire for her took every ounce of self-control he possessed.

As he had sat next to her wiping his dagger on his pants, he had wondered if she noticed what was going on between his legs. He thought about slicing his own dick off, imagining it would be less painful than the bite from his zipper and the humiliation of her knowing his desire for her. She hated him, but he could never hate her, even though he'd acted like an ass.

He took the steps two at a time down to his apartment floor. The door unlocked with a click after he placed his hand on the bio-scanner. In the middle of his quarters sat a king-sized mattress and box-spring bed. No headboard, only a small side table and lamp. The gray blanket was still rumpled in the middle with a flat pillow. He headed right for the bathroom, not bothering to shut the door behind him. Zaan, one of the many cats living at Headquarters, trotted in after him. He was one of the few male felines, and had claimed Dru as his. Purring, he rubbed against his shins.

"I missed you too."

Zaan sat and stared up at him.

"You'll never guess who I saw tonight."

Meow.

"Yeah, how'd you know?" Dru smirked. "Kalani. Yeah, I know what you're thinking, she hates me."

He always spoke to the cats in the building as if they understood English. With how they behaved, maybe they did. He was positive his best friend Riordan's cat was a wizardess.

He undressed, turned on the shower, and stepped under the spray. Water ran over his body, washing away the dried, dark purple demon blood. The phosphorescence had faded. Dru soaped up and shampooed his hair. He scrubbed with a soapy washcloth until his skin turned red.

His thoughts drifted to Kalani. Rob had seemed interested in her. What was she doing with a human? Dru wanted to choke him to death, even though it wasn't the guy's fault. He never thought of himself as having homicidal tendencies toward humans.

After turning off the water, Dru dried himself, wrapped the terrycloth towel around his waist, and returned to the bedroom. That was when the silent alarm went off. The Bator who lived here rotated tending to any alarm triggers. A light by the door near the ceiling flashed red, which meant an alarm had been set off in the drainage system. The flashing light changed to yellow, indicating someone had entered the ventilation shaft. Great. Only a Bator possessed immunity to the sleep gas in the main tunnel. The shit had a metallic scent, not unlike blood. Although Red had a stronger coppery smell.

Whoever had gotten past the gas was Bator and small enough to fit through the ventilation shafts.

Kalani...

Dru plugged his legs into a pair of nylon track pants and put on a pair of Nikes. He grabbed a dagger on the way out, just in case the intruder wasn't Kalani. The building had two elevator shafts, only one had a working car, and the other was an empty straight shot to the basement floors, ideal for vaping. He opened the elevator shaft without the car and vaped down to a small platform outside the sliding doors of the floor where the ventilation shafts led. After pressing his hand to the bio-scanner, the doors retracted.

Angling his head, he listened for the intruder. Glass crashed to the floor. Dru crept down the hall to his left on the balls of his shoes. Thirty feet from the Red Dispensary Room, he smelled her. His body instantly hardened. What the hell? He sucked in a breath. Big mistake, because he received an even larger dose of Kalani's scent. More glass broke, which he now knew were blood vials. More hit the linoleum one by one in rapid succession.

CRASH! BOOM!

That didn't sound good. Dru ran for the Dispensary.

Inside the room, Kalani was crouched on her hands and knees, licking Red straight from the tile.

Glass shards littered the floor all around her. Next to her lay one entire wall cooling unit, the doors of which had been torn off and tossed aside.

When was the last time she drank any blood? When she was sixteen?

"Lani!"

She snarled, warning him to stay back.

Dru ignored her, stomping forward, glass crunching under his Nikes. "Lani!"

A growl ripped out of her throat.

"Kalani! Stop!" At the rate she was consuming the Red, she would be high on the stuff for days. She looked up but kept lapping at the blood. Her eyes still had those stupid contacts in them. Holding her down and removing the damn things crossed his mind. "You're gonna get sick if you don't quit it."

"I need it!" Blood covered her chin, dripping onto the floor.

"No. You don't." He yanked her off the floor by the waist. She kicked and screamed. "Shhh! Do you want the Director to hear you? He's only one floor above this room."

"I don't care. Let me go!" Her foot connected with his shin and Dru groaned.

"Well, I do." He carried her out of the room and down the hallway with his hand clamped over her mouth. She continued yelling, although the sounds were muffled. Pressing the bio-scanner to open the elevator doors posed a problem. "I'm going to uncover your mouth. Do you think you can behave yourself for a minute?"

She sighed heavily through her nose and nodded.

He released her mouth.

"You ass—"

Dru coved her mouth again. "Be quiet—ow!" She'd bit him. "Are you kidding me? I have to take you upstairs before someone wanders down here and sees you." He shook his hand out. Her incisors had left two holes in his index finger.

"Stop covering my mouth then."

"Stop screaming then and...*biting* me. You're lucky I don't bite you back."

"Try it," she said between clenched teeth. "See what happens."

"Oh yeah, my *fangs* are bigger." Dru chomped the air, making a snapping noise with his teeth. He pressed his hand to the glass plate and the doors slid wide. Without putting her down, he got in the elevator.

Just as the doors closed, Director Cutler appeared in the narrow gap, looking pissed. "Druit!" The car lurched upward.

"You can put me down now," Kalani said.

"No. I don't trust you."

"You have no idea how much I hate you manhandling me."

"I haven't seen you in almost ten years, how can you hate it already?"

Or is it that you hate me touching you?

"What?"

"You know what? Maybe if I didn't have to pry you off the floor like some blood-crazed lunatic I would. My gods, you were licking it off the floor."

"It spilled. What was I supposed to do, waste it?" She squirmed in his arms. The underside of his stiff cock nestled into the crack of her ass.

Dru's breath caught in the back of his throat. "Uh."

"What's the matter with you?"

Did she seriously not feel what was pressed against her bottom? His junk was free range in his pants, after all. Was she trying to insult him? "Nothing. You're irritating me."

"*Pfft.* I'm sure that's true. You're poking me."

Dru coughed and choked a bit on his saliva. He *wished* he was poking her and a whole lot more. Nearly forgetting the English language, he didn't respond.

* * *

Kalani

Despite the sarcastic bickering with Dru, Kalani

couldn't keep her mind off Red. Yes, she knew he was hard for her, but she didn't care about that. Nor was she interested in dealing right now. The scent of his blood distracted her from everything. If only she could turn around.

"Please let me go, I promise I won't scream."

"Uh uh," he grunted.

"Please..." she begged, near tears. His hold eased, allowing her toes to touch the floor. She swiveled in his arms and faced him. He looked over the top of her head, his expression stony. The jugular vein in his neck pulsed. Oh God, a feast at eye level. Her mouth watered and her tongue swelled. She swallowed hard and licked her lips. "D-Dru," her voice wavered, "I need—"

"I loosened my grip. What more—"

Kalani shoved him back against the wall of the elevator and climbed up his body, clinging to his waist and shoulders. Her fangs imbedded in his neck.

"Fuck. Lani, not here..." His words held no conviction or threat of later retaliation for the personal violation. She had him at first glance back on that highway. As if she hadn't noticed his erection—no amount of leather could hide what he had going on in his pants.

He ran a hand up the back of her neck, his warm

fingers caressing her. It was almost...sweet. Tender. He wanted her there too...

"Ouch!" Dru's fingers clamped down, pinching her neck to the point of serious pain. Tears welling in her eyes, Kalani retracted her teeth from his throat.

"You need to stop, you'll get sick."

She placed her feet on the floor while a tear slid down her cheek. Why was she crying? What was she upset about? That he had physically subdued her or she wanted more blood?

The elevator stopped a moment later. She stared at his chest. For the first time, she realized he was shirtless. What a gorgeous chest. He didn't look like this ten years ago. He'd been sixteen then, but still. Her mouth watered for a different reason now. Damn him. And damn her for what she was thinking of doing.

CHAPTER FIVE

DRU

Gah! This was turning out to be the worst night. He hated himself for using pain to make her stop feeding off him and for loving what she had been doing in the first place.

The tears she shed, the quiver in her chin. They were his fault.

"I'm—"

No. He wasn't going to apologize, she should have controlled herself. Oh, what the hell was he saying? He loved it and wanted her to take more from him. The mere thought turned him on, stirring feelings he wanted to suppress. Most Bator didn't have sex with other Bator. A screw you to the creators, pregnancies, even accidental pregnancies, between Bator made the scientists happy. A Bator created not in a lab but by natural means made their work easier. You would think the opposite would be true. This always baffled Dru. Perhaps they wanted to harvest stem cells or some shit for making the next generation of Bator. He didn't know though.

Kalani took a deep breath. The doors opened and Dru expected the director to be standing there waiting. He peeked around the doors. The hallway was empty in both directions. He took her hand and led her to his room. She remained unusually quiet.

Dru opened the door, allowing her to enter first. She kept her eyes trained on the floor as she sat on the bed. Zaan jumped to the floor and scurried under the bed.

"All right. What's wrong?"

Kalani looked at him. A streak of dried blood ran from one corner of her mouth to her chin. She swiped at a single tear on her cheek then rubbed the back of her neck. He had needed to use more force than should have been necessary to subdue her. She hadn't felt his hand until his knuckles turned white.

"Nothing." She rubbed her eyes then remembered the contacts and dropped her hand.

"How's your neck?"

Kalani sniffed. "Why do you care?"

"Let me see your neck. I have something I can put on it." Confusion washed over her features. "For the bruising."

"You didn't pinch that hard." He came forward and lifted the hair off her neck. She arched her back and pulled away. "I don't know why you insist on touching me."

He held his hands up in surrender. "Suit yourself, just trying to be nice."

"For once."

Dru frowned. *What does that mean?*

"I am nice," he said.

"Whatever." She stood, crossing her arms over her chest.

"You know, you can just say fuck off instead. We both know that's what you mean to say anyway."

"Fuck off."

He couldn't tell if she was looking at him or not with those contacts in her eyes. It seemed as if she was staring through him or somewhere off in space. "Take those things out of your eyes. I can't even look at you like that."

"What things?"

"You know what things. Take them out." He enunciated the "T."

"No. They help me see."

Dru rolled his eyes. "Gimme a break, you have better than 20/20 vision."

"No, I don't. I have terrible vision."

"Yeah, maybe with those stupid things in your eyes. Take them out."

"No."

"Take them out or I won't help you find your friend." He didn't plan on helping, but she didn't know that.

"What makes you think that's why I'm here?"

"Oh, it isn't, huh?" Dru ground his molars, his jaw tightening.

"I came to see you."

Dru chuckled. "Yeah, okay. Had you been planning to find me before or after you destroyed the Dispensary?"

"That was an accident."

He sighed heavily. "You've got to be kidding me," he muttered. A hard knock at the door resounded. He threw a glance in Kalani's direction that she mistook as a warning.

"Where do I hide?" she whispered, racing around the room searching for a place to hide.

"What are you doing?"

"Hiding."

"Who's there?" Dru asked, standing right behind the door.

"Dru," she said, waving her hands frantically.

He turned toward the door. "I don't know where you think you're going to hide. This is a small ass apartment. Besides, Cutler already knows you're here."

There was another knock at the door followed by, "Dru?" The voice wasn't the Director's. He cracked the door and let Riordan in. Kalani had disappeared, although she hadn't gone far. He still sensed her.

Riordan entered, sniffed the air, and turned back in Dru's direction. "What the hell did you do?"

Dru shrugged. "Gotta be a little more specific than that.

Riordan chuckled. "You know you're out of your mind." He walked around the room, checked under the bed, in the closet. "I take it she's in the bathroom?"

"Who?"

"Oh, come on, the female Bator. I can smell her."

Dru crossed his arms over his chest. "I don't know what you're talking about."

Riordan rolled his eyes. "Cutler's pissed. What the hell happened?"

"Some rats got in the ventilation shaft."

"Oh so, *rats* knocked over one of the coolers in the Dispensary? Those are some big fucking rats. And explain how they got past the sleep gas, hmm?" Riordan laughed.

"What can I say?" Dru laughed with him.

"So who is she?"

"She used to be in the program a long time ago but chose to leave."

Riordan raised his eyebrows. "Ah, well, she should probably leave before Cutler finds her in your room."

"I know. She's leaving soon."

"Why don't you take her to the roof so she can vape?"

Dru shook his head.

"You mean...you mean she can't vape? Wow. A Bator who can resist the Red cravings?"

"Who do you think knocked over the cooler? So I'd say no. Once her strength returns and she can vape, she's leaving."

"Good luck with that. Now, I gotta go clean her mess up." Riordan headed for the door. "Oh, by the way, Cutler did send me up here to get rid of her, but—"

"Thanks, I owe you."

Riordan sighed. "Just make sure she's gone by morning, all right? Or you know it's my ass."

The bathroom door flew open. "Riory?" Kalani

said. "Is that you?" She rushed him and threw her arms around his neck.

"Kalani? Oh my gods." A wide grin spread across this face.

* * *

Kalani

"I can't believe it, you've gotten so big. The last time I saw you...oh my God," Kalani said. She hadn't seen Riordan since he was around twelve years old.

He chuckled. "Well, I'm twenty-two now. I've changed."

"I can see that. You look good, I hardly recognized you." She stepped back and looked him up and down. It occurred to her that males always did this move, as if females didn't know they were being checked out. Kalani recognized his scent before his face. However, he still had the chiseled good looks and dimple in one of his cheeks. His dark blond hair flopped over his forehead, and of course his eyes were the same color as all Bator. She disliked the term Bator. It was short for incubator. She and the rest of her kind spent many months in clear-plastic cages, or tanks, as Dru had referred to them, with tubes sticking out of their tiny bodies. They started out in artificial wombs resembling fish tanks then graduated to fluid free cages after the umbilical cord was no longer needed.

Dru cleared his throat, snapping her back to the present.

Riordan embraced her again. She imagined his body was as ripped as Dru's underneath the sweats and hoodie. He held her longer than necessary, to the point she wondered if he'd let go. Riordan released his hold and backed away a few feet.

Dru stepped up and loomed behind her, heat radiating off him.

Somebody's jealous.

What a wasted emotion. Or was it? She put a finger up to her lips. Hmm, wait a minute... Kalani breathed deeply but quietly. Jealously could help her if she still wasn't able to vape. Although she had some Red, Dru had stopped her well before her fill.

"Don't you have somewhere to be?" Dru asked Riordan. His voice sounded predatory.

"Yeah," Riordan said, keeping his eyes trained on her. "I gotta go clean Kalani's—"

"Oh!" She slapped her hands over her mouth. "I'm so sorry. I should help you."

Dru furrowed his brow. "No. You shouldn't."

"He's right, not a good idea. Are we going to be seeing more of you around?" Riordan's face brightened. His attraction for her was obvious in his expression, and the way he puffed his chest.

"That depends. Are you leaving the Patrol Guard?"

God, he turned out cute.

Oh, what was she thinking about? He used to follow her around like a lost puppy. She feared this wouldn't change. And what a turn off. Riordan also had a human-like quality to his personality, a more lower-on-the-food-chain mentality, less apex predator. Dru dripped with a raw sexiness Riordan lacked. He oozed sex.

"No," he said, blushing.

"You'll have to *come* visit me sometime." Okay, now she was *trying* to make Dru jealous. She needed his blood and this was the only way she saw to get it.

Riordan's jaw dropped. "Ah...um..." He swallowed hard.

Despite their obvious friendship, Dru shoved Riordan toward the door. "Isn't it time for you to leave?"

Riordan careened into the door shoulder first. He caught himself from faceplanting into the thing by placing his hands on the metal panel. "Hey, take it easy."

"Out," Dru barked. "And don't forget to clean that mess downstairs."

Kalani folded her arms across her chest. "Why are you being such a dick?"

"Seriously, man, you're being an ass," Riordan said.

Dru shot her a look, and a quick, sharp snarl, the timbre of which surprised her. Bator had an array of sounds that meant specific things. Humans tended not to hear the subtle differences or understand the nuances. This was a non-verbal communication only Bator understood instinctually, and the sound wasn't shut-up-you're-irritating-me. It meant this-is-my-territory-and-everything-in-it-is-mine-including-you.

Kalani closed her eyes. Damn. She had done it this time. What a stupid plan. She hadn't really thought through the consequences of what she'd schemed. By making him jealous of Riordan, she believed he'd fall into bed with her so she could feed. In theory, Bator blood would make her strong enough to rescue Jade. But things never quite went as planned, did they? Clearly she had spent way too much time with human men, who were easily manipulated and didn't form bonds with females. Now it was only a matter of time before she wouldn't be able to leave him. The bond worked both ways. She had maybe a day or two before she needed to possess Dru as much as he did her.

Hang on Jade...

CHAPTER SIX

DRU

Dru gripped Riordan by the nape of his neck and slammed him into the door. "I told you to leave."

"I am. I am. What's your problem?" Riordan fumbled for the door handle, looking over his shoulder at Kalani. The other male wore a worried expression. However, his own safety was in jeopardy, not hers.

Only dimly aware of his actions, Dru set his feet and body into a ready-to-pounce stance. He curled his upper lip, showing off his fangs. "Get out," he growled.

"I am!" Riordan cranked the door open, exited, and slammed it in Dru's face.

Dru punched the door with his fist.

The most delicious noise escaped Kalani's mouth, a cross between a whimper and a gasp. The sound only meant one thing to Bator. He snapped his head in her direction. "What was that?"

She kicked up her chin. "Nothing."

"I think it was something." Gods, the noise she made. His body tingled.

"No, it wasn't, I don't know what you're talking about."

"I know what I heard." She wanted him.

"Then why did you ask me?"

"I want you too."

"What makes you think I want you?"

"You can't fake that sound."

"Sure I can. Females do it all the time." Kalani crossed her arms over her chest.

Dru smirked. "Yeah, who have you faked it with? A human." Stalking toward her, he gripped the waistband of his track pants. His body buzzed with anticipation. Her eyes flared and the same noise came out again. She slapped a hand over her mouth.

"Take the contacts out. I want to see your eyes." Without taking his eyes off her, he pulled his pants down and stepped out of them.

"What in the hell are you doing? Put your pants back on." Kalani moved around to the other side of the bed, although she kept staring at what was between his legs.

"Your playing-hard-to-get routine is ridiculous."

"I am hard to get."

"And I'm hard."

"You amuse me. See? I'm laughing at you." She tilted her head back while faking a laugh.

He snort-chuckled. She looked adorable bluffing. "Take your clothes off."

"What...is wrong with you?"

"Not a thing. Take your clothes off. Please." Yes. For the first time, everything was right. The timing sucked though. He knew she'd likely screw him over after this, but he'd deal with that later. Dru wasn't an idiot. She had come here for Red so she could help her friend. Yet she'd leave with so much more.

Kalani stared at him for a minute. "I think I may hate you."

"Fair enough. You can brood later."

"Arghhh! You're impossible." She threw her hands up. "I said I hate you."

"No. You *may* hate me is what you said."

Her eyes narrowed. "What. Ever."

"If you don't want me, why do you keep making that noise?"

"I'm faking it." She fingered the hem of her shirt.

"Not possible. But before you take your shirt off, remove the lenses."

"Who said I was taking my shirt off?" The last word was muffled by the cloth going over her head. The shirt hit the floor.

Dru's lips parted and he sucked in a breath. "Then how come it's on the floor?"

"You're craz—uh! What the..." Covering her bare breasts, she glanced around the room.

"Put your hands down. I already saw your tits." And they were fantastic. Dru knelt on the bed. "Come here."

She moved toward him and the bed. "I'm scared."

"Of what? And for the record, I don't believe you."

"It's true, I've never been with another Bator."

"Whose fault is that? And I still think you're full of shit."

"Fine, I'm not scared, but I seriously haven't been with our kind before, you know."

He reached for her. "I'll be gentle your first time. You're gonna want to take out the contacts though."

"Why?" Kalani grasped his hand after a slight

hesitation. When she'd paused, he wondered if she was telling the truth about being afraid.

"Just trust me."

"I do," she whispered almost inaudibly as if she hadn't wanted him to hear. With her hair swept over to one side, she looked like the teenager he once knew. Except her breasts were fuller and her hips flared more, giving her an hourglass shape.

After she climbed on the bed and laid down, he worked the rest of her clothes off. He settled between her thighs, hovering inches above her body. "Contacts. Out."

"You win." She plucked the lenses out and flicked them off her fingers.

Finally, he could see her irises. The slit pupils were dilated. Bator had the same basic color eyes, but variations occurred, like how blue eyes differed from one human to the next.

Reaching up, she stroked his cheek and passed her thumb across his lips. He opened his mouth and kissed the pad of her finger. She closed her eyes and moaned softly.

His blood surged south. "Lani," he breathed.

"I know, I want you too."

Yes. His arms weakened, and he laid on top of her, their skin making contact for the first time. Her skin burned. The orange of her eyes glowed brighter. So beautiful...

Dipping his head, he pressed his lips to hers. She returned the kiss. Dru began slowly devouring, savoring, claiming what was his. No other female would do now and this was before they even had sex.

Kalani rocked her hips. He growled into the crook of her neck. "Oh, Lani..."

She giggled. "What was that?"

"Do you know what you do to me?" Dru captured her hands by weaving their fingers together and put them over her head. The fire in her eyes flared.

"Oh, I think I might."

* * *

Kalani

Oh, I think I might.

What was she saying? She should be running from the room, with the way he held her hands over her head. The mere thought of surrendering to a male, regardless of the species, frightened her. Made her feel like going on a homicidal rampage. She was an independent woman. Dammit! Shit... Bator. Woman was a human term. But she welcomed his possession of her—nearly had an orgasm in anticipation.

No. No, no, no. She wasn't interested in him.

All right, she was. But this wasn't what this was about. Kalani needed to save Jade. That was the only objective here. Dru's blood would help her do it. He had already made it clear he wasn't rescuing her best friend. He was probably right, make that most definitely right, that she couldn't be saved. Jade would be used by the Collective who stole her, draining her blood until she was half dead, over and over for however long her human body could withstand. Even if Kalani freed Jade, the damage may be too great for her to make a full recovery.

"Dru, you can drink from me if you want."

He sank his fangs into her neck. She allowed him to drink from her because she knew he'd reciprocate without questioning her motives. Dru wasn't stupid. However, to get her friend back, she wasn't above using manipulation. Allowing her muscles to relax, she sagged beneath him, opening her legs wider.

"Drink," she whispered. He sucked harder, tightening the hold on her hands. She squeezed back. Tears sprang to her eyes. Although he wasn't hurting her, she imagined the future hurt she'd bestow upon him.

Dru shifted, angled his hips, and pushed inside her. Kalani gasped. "Oh...oh..." Feelings of completeness filled her soul. A sensation of floating overcame her, except when she looked around, they were still on the bed.

Panic hit her square in the chest. She stiffened. Dru's fangs retracted, and the wound self-sealed, a result of his saliva and Bator's rapid cell regeneration process. He lifted his head and stilled for a moment. "What's wrong? Did I hurt you?"

The floating feeling disappeared. She shook her head.

"Are you sure? Was it the floaty feeling?"

"You felt it too?"

"Yes, it's normal."

Normal?

How was that normal? That never happened during sex with humans. Gah! She wasn't a human by *human* standards. Sure, they were part human, and Bator looked and sounded like humans. Mostly sounded like humans. They could talk, but the array of growls and purrs set them apart. And they drank blood.

"You don't believe me?" he asked, moving inside her again. Ecstasy rolled through her. What had she been thinking about? Hell if she knew.

Oh, floaty thing. Sex with humans with no floaty thing.

Which was better? Oh God, Bator sex. Bator sex was soooo much better. Dru thrust deep, driving her further into the mattress. Sweat pooled between her breasts. His chest rumbled, vibrating against hers.

"Dru!" she screamed. He released her hands and flipped them over, putting her on top.

Turning his head to the side he said, "Drink." When she didn't lunge for his throat, he pushed her forward with a knee. Her hands went to his chest, holding her up. She licked her lips, attempting to quell her dry mouth. His vein pulsed inches from her mouth. Her fangs descended.

Thirsty.

So thirsty. She swirled her hips and his head tilted back, letting out a roar. The sight may have been the sexiest thing she had ever seen. He was giving himself to her, and what was she about to do? Destroy him by taking his blood and leaving. She would go but she wasn't going to take Red from him too, not like this. Somehow it seemed worse than what had happened in the elevator.

Kalani clutched his shoulders and rode him hard. She kept her mouth away from his throat and enjoyed the sensations of her building orgasm. Their breaths sawed in and out to the rhythm of their bodies. Her heart beat faster. The bed quaked beneath them to the point she wanted to hold it down, but it wasn't the bed, it was them climaxing together.

"Oh, God! Yes!" she hollered. And then...

The door burst open.

CHAPTER SEVEN

KALANI

BOOM!

The door flew open, lodging the handle in the drywall behind it. Dru flipped her over, withdrew, and backed off the bed, pushing the blanket toward her.

Cutler and Dru prowled around each other like animals. The director purred, sounding like low, gruff clicks in the back of his throat. A show of controlled anger. For now, anyway.

"She's mine," Dru's bass voice cut through the room. He wiped blood from the corner of his mouth.

"You didn't ask my permission," Cutler snarled.

"I don't need your permission."

"Yes. You. Do."

"I can mate with whoever I want."

"Agreed."

"What?"

"I meant she doesn't have permission to enter these premises. Plus, she ruined the lab."

Hardly. One cooler, Kalani thought.

"Hardly. It was one fucking cooler."

What the what?

Was Dru already linked to her? He'd certainly taken enough of her blood, except the link required her to drink from him too. *Oh...*Her hand went her mouth. *Uh oh*. How could she have forgotten about the elevator so quickly? Bator orgasm. It was the only explanation for losing her damn mind. Kalani gathered her clothes and shrank away from the males. She stood near the door getting dressed.

"One big fucking cooler and a whole mess of wasted Red," Cutler snarled.

"So?" Dru said.

"It was a six-week supply."

The males continued arguing about whether she stayed. Kalani made the choice easy for them both and slipped out the door.

She ran down the hallway on the balls of her feet. Closing her eyes, she concentrated on vaping but nothing happened. Damn. More Red was needed and fast. Riordan's scent lingered near the stairwell. The metal door was secured with a bio-scanner. These contraptions had been installed after her departure from the program. Just for the hell of it, she placed her hand on the glass plate. What was it detecting? Actual fingerprints or Bator DNA? It was a bio scanner, after all.

The lock clicked, disengaging. She hit the release bar and took the steps two at a time. Riordan's scent led her up to the roof. At the top of the stairs, the access door was propped open. She bumped the fire extinguisher that had kept it from closing.

Riordan sat on one of the gargoyles. When the door slammed, he spun and jumped to his feet, ready for an attack. He'd changed out of the sweats from earlier into part of the Patrol Guard's chosen uniform, black leather pants and boots. The black hoodie remained, although now unzipped halfway down. "Damn, Kalani, you startled me."

"Sorry."

"Where's Dru?"

"Sleeping. I didn't want to wake him. I have to get home before Cutler finds me."

He grinned. "Good idea."

Closing her eyes, she tried vaping again. Still nothing. How much Red would it take? The shit spilled on the floor in her bloodthirsty hunt and the amount she had taken from Dru in the elevator hadn't been enough.

Riordan leapt off the statue. The jugulars in his neck pulsed. Cotton filled her mouth. She stared at the vein on his right side.

"Kalani?"

"Huh?"

"I asked if you were all right."

"Oh, I'm fine." She shook her head, her eyes focused on his throat. He stepped up to her, requiring her to look at his face. Around his neck, he wore a black hemp choker with three turquoise beads braided into it. "Is that the necklace I made for you when we were kids?"

"Yeah," he blushed. "It's tighter now."

"A lot tighter. I can't believe you kept it."

Riordan shrugged. "I like it."

She stood on her tippy toes and kissed his left cheek. "That's very sweet of you." The Bator training and education program had a mandatory arts and crafts class.

Cue the eyeball roll, please.

He stood stock still when she brushed another kiss on his right cheek. "I bet you taste good," she whispered, running her lips down his neck. He gasped, swallowing. Her fangs descended. She'd end up in Hell for this. Good thing she was headed there anyway. The demon Collectives' realm probably *was* Hell for all anybody knew.

Kalani struck his vein like a cobra. Hard. Lightening quick.

He groaned, "What are you doing?"

Kalani couldn't explain with a mouthful of blood. The reason wasn't exactly sane, either. She drank until the beginnings of the vaporization process started. Her molecules shrank and separated into a fine mist, starting from the rooftop to her head.

CHAPTER EIGHT

DRU

Dru curled his hands into fists as he faced off with Cutler. "Let's ask Kalani what she wants to do."

The director seethed. "Fine. But she pays for the damages." After ten minutes of arguing, neither of them backing off, Dru had worn Cutler down. The male understood how bond mates worked and ultimately wouldn't interfere, even if Kalani had broken into the building. Perhaps in the back of his mind, he believed she might join the Patrol Guard again.

"Thank you." Dru smiled crookedly.

"Yeah, yeah," Cutler waved him off, looking around the apartment. "Hey, where is she?"

Dru's heart froze. She was gone. Bator blood had a tracer signature that echoed back like sonar when the donor was within two miles, and it picked up nothing. There wasn't any lingering vapor either. He blew out a breath.

"Are you picking anything up?" Cutler asked.

"Fuck." Dru winced.

"Stay here."

"She probably went home."

Cutler stormed out of the apartment. Dru slammed the door shut behind the Bator. He grabbed his cell phone off the night stand and sent a text to Riordan.

Dru: U home?

Dru dressed then started pacing before he got a return text.

Riordan: Roof.

Although he'd been told to stay, fuck that. Finding Kalani needed to happen now. Her going into the Collective realm by herself was suicide. Hell, even with the whole Patrol Guard it would be insane.

Dru vaped down the hallway and up the stairs to the rooftop. No one was on the roof, at least that was what he thought at first. He found Riordan leaning against the side of the concrete stairwell housing in the shadows. "What are you doing back there?"

"Taking a breather."

"From what? Did you go on a thirty second mission?"

"No, smart-ass."

At the same time, they both said, "Kalani's gone."

"How do you know?" Dru asked. Riordan remained against the building, his face in shadow. "What's wrong with you?"

"She tricked me. For a second I thought she digged me."

"What happened?"

Shit.

Dru didn't want his friend to say it. He knew she had drank from Riordan.

"She tapped your fucking vein, didn't she?" Anger rose from his gut. "Godammit!"

"I'm sorry."

"Never mind that, where is she?"

"I lost trac—"

"Why didn't you follow her?"

Riordan stepped away from the wall and into

the light from the fixture over the roof access door. "Didn't you feed her?"

"Not enough for her to vape," Dru bit out.

"Maybe she wanted to go home."

"Not. She came here for Red and I caught her in the Dispensary, remember?"

"Oh. I thought—wait, she came here for Red? Why?"

"Her friend Jade was taken tonight."

Riordan tilted his head back. "Aw, fuck."

"Yep."

"You don't think...?"

"Yep."

"That's crazy. They'll kill her if they catch her in their realm."

"No shit. Now you see why I need to find her. We're wasting time."

Riordan closed his eyes and breathed deeply. "I lost her signal north of here, come on."

* * *

Kalani

Kalani reformed out of a swirling black cloud of vapor inside the gas station where Benny had dropped her off. She didn't bother concealing her magic trick. Jojo, the station's owner, dove behind the counter. He bounced up a moment later holding his hands up like a surgeon preparing for a nurse to put gloves on him.

Demons had mysophobia, the fear of dirt. She wasn't all that thrilled about it, either. She refused to believe it was because of her demon side. Jojo wore brown contacts hiding the purple. Despite the lenses, he had on sunglasses—the florescent overhead lights hurt his eyes, as did the daylight.

"You really need to learn to relax," Kalani chided. "When have I ever come after you?"

"There's always a first time."

"You still connected?"

Jojo sucked in a tense breath. "Always. Why?"

"Can you tell me where the portal is?"

The gateways shifted like weather, or at least it seemed that way. There was probably some unseen force controlling these things. Bator had never figured it out. Random was the best word to describe the shifting pattern.

"How does that work? Does your Collective leave you alone or do—"

"As much as I hate the Collective, I can't tell you shit."

"Jade was taken."

"And they are?"

Kalani looked at him cross-eyed. "Don't play

stupid, you know who she is." He should, Jojo hit on her every time they came in here.

"I can't tell you if I want to keep my head."

"Not even for Jade?"

"I can't."

Kalani exhaled, sagging her shoulders. She didn't want to use intimidation to get an involuntary confession. Jojo was what Bator called a "good demon." And relatively weak-minded for one. She'd have to press him to think about the Collective portal, then he'd show her the location without opening his mouth. She wasn't sure how long her energy would last and digging into his mind would be an energy zapper. Kalani didn't have any time to waste. "Just remember, you made me to do this."

"I can't—No!"

She threw herself at him, her body half vaping to clear the counter. Grabbing him by the throat, she slammed him into the racks behind him. Cartons of cigarettes nailed him in the head. He tried head-butting her, but she dodged the attack.

A roar ripped out of his mouth. Chimes over the door jangled as customers fled.

"Make as much noise as you want, I'll still get what I want." She caught his throat again and squeezed, pressing her thumbs into his windpipe.

"Awk." Jojo's eyes bulged.

"Where is it?"

He shook his head. "Awk, awk..."

"Where. Is. It? And I'll let you go." Kalani wasn't planning on murdering the demon, only scaring him a little. Well, a lot actually. Whatever it took to see the portal's location.

She tunneled into Jojo's mind, wading through what he ate for breakfast three days ago, his last date, oh God, that wasn't something she could unsee...

Finally, she saw what she had been after. The demon showed her a place. Nothing special, but an area a few miles from the gas station. "A park." Kalani knew exactly where it was.

He shook his head.

"What do you mean, no?" She eased her hands off his throat.

"I don't know about any park." Jojo's voice sounded gravely.

"Why think of it then?" If Kalani was him she wouldn't be thinking of a place she'd never been while someone choked her. The mind was a funny thing, if you tried not thinking about something, you always thought about it more.

"Please...I don't know—"

She flashed her fangs, ready to tear his throat out.

"I don't know Johnson Park—fuck!"

A smile crept across her face. "Thank you." She

vaped, releasing his neck right before completely disappearing.

The power surging throughout her body heightened her senses. The stars lit the sky. Bator saw millions of colors, even more than tetrachromat humans, Johnson Park was a children's playground during the day. Although Kalani couldn't find the Collective portal, her DNA allowed her entry. If only she could find the invisible gateway.

In the middle of the empty park sat a large wooden play structure with slides and plastic covered tunnels. Beyond that was a swing set she couldn't see entirely behind the monstrosity in front of her.

Trees lined the outer edges of the park. The branches were still and their leaves didn't rustle in the breezeless night.

Squeak. Squeak. Squeeeeak...

Kalani spun. What the hell?

Squeak... The sound came from the other side of the play structure. She ran toward the noise. A lone swing swayed in the middle of a row. She grabbed the chains, steadying them. The rubber seat twisted, continuing to move even though she held the links. The swing acted as a divining rod, pointing toward the portal.

"Found you," she hissed.

Heading in the direction the swing was pulled

in, Kalani took deep, calming breaths. They didn't work on easing her nerves, though. She suddenly wondered why she even considered doing this alone. In truth, she couldn't ask Dru to throw away his job for one woman. Really? No way had Kalani believed that. It was more like she asked him to commit suicide. How could she blame him for refusing? Wait, had he refused?

Stop that. You're doing this.

The ends of her hair sucked out in front of her. She inched toward the portal. A magnetic force yanked her forward. Humans passing the gateway weren't affected by the sucking vortex, only those with demon blood.

The Collectives' voices grew louder until all she heard was them. No single voice stood out among the thousands. The fragmented bits Kalani had made out sounded like thoughts as opposed to conversations between the demons. Fortunately, the din could be tuned out like white noise.

She took longer strides as the sucking got stronger. Glancing over her shoulder, she discovered the swing more than twenty feet away now.

No going back.

Holding her breath because it seemed the right thing to do, Kalani's body lifted from the ground. "Oh, shit!"

She floated to the opening, not that she saw it,

but she sensed it was there. With her hands out, Kalani broke through the fissure in the gateway into...

She dropped to the ground. At first, she thought she was still in the park. That quickly changed.

CHAPTER NINE

DRU

Dru was aware of violating the order from Director Cutler to stay put. Did he care? Nope, not especially. Twenty-four hours ago he would have never even considered it though. Except, Kalani needed him. Not that she wanted his help. Again, did he care? Not an ounce.

Riordan had been able to pinpoint her last

location. More than likely she was out of range by now. They vaped to a gas station owned by a known demon. Jojo. Fucking Jojo. All right, the guy was okay, for a demon. Dru looked through the glass door. The "good" demon, meaning one that chose not to remain part of a Collective, stacked cartons of cigarettes on a shelf behind the counter.

Dru reached into the urn next to the door filled with cigarette butts and dirty sand, grabbing a fistful. He coughed and averted his head away from offending shit. "Ew...gawd..."

Riordan shivered. "How can you touch that filth?"

"It's not easy, believe me." Everyone had their own methods of interrogation. With full-blooded demons, only one worked best. Anything dirty. Dru gagged. Riordan opened the door for him and entered the gas station behind Dru.

Jojo's eyes widened and he dropped a carton of Marlboro Reds. He bolted.

Riordan vaped into his path. "Where are you going so fast?"

"Nowhere," Jojo said, backing up.

"We want to talk," Dru said in the demon's right ear, who shied away from him.

"I got nothing to say."

"But you don't know what I want to talk to you about," Dru drawled. In a fight ready stance, he dipped his head forward, glaring at the gas station owner.

"Whatever it is, I don't know any—"

Riordan bear hugged Jojo from behind, falling backward with him and slamming the demon onto the tile. The demon moaned and rolled from side to side.

Dru slapped Jojo's cheek, knocking sunglasses off his face. "Listen up, I'm only going to ask you this once. Where did you send the female Bator?"

"W-what Bator?"

Dru clutched the demon's jaw, holding his fist with the butts and sand over his mouth.

Jojo shook his head violently. "No. No..." A cigarette butt and a few grains of sand hit his lips. He squirmed. Tears formed in his eyes.

"Oh, come on, it's not that bad. Where did you send her?"

"I don't know what you're talking about," Jojo spat.

"We know she was here."

"Not tonight."

Dru dropped another butt, this one with a lipstick ring. Jojo flinched and whimpered.

"You want this to stop?"

The demon blinked tears out of his eyes. Dru flipped him over, sunk a knee into his back, and pressed his cheek to the floor. He put the remaining dirty sand on the tile in front of Jojo's face. Riordan stayed ready for anything.

"Where did you send her?" Dru picked up a butt.

"I didn't send Kalani anywhere," Jojo blurted.

"Who mentioned her name?" Dru asked. "Riordan, did you say her name?"

"Nope, sure didn't. *Tsk, tsk, tsk.* Where did you send her?"

Dru had been zeroing in on the demon's thoughts, who so far had avoided showing him where he'd sent Kalani. Saying her name, however, sparked a stronger image. "Johnson Park. Thank you."

Riordan mouthed, *one...two...* On three, the Bator vaped to the park.

Chapter Ten

KALANI

Kalani landed in deep grass. Up in the sky hung what looked like an oversized eclipsed sun. Underneath her bottom, the sod had the same feel as the grass on Earth. What struck her as odd was the color of the blades. They had an eerie hue, as if they were glowing.

What kind of alien grass is this?

In the dim light, something long, thin, and dark parted the grass, slithering toward her. She gasped, realizing it was a snake. What light there was highlighted its black scales. The snake raised a portion of its body, baring its fangs.

She bounded to her feet and took off running. A large rock formation loomed ahead of her in the distance. The peak resembled a pyramid. With nothing else in sight, she headed there, hoping she could find shelter inside.

Some type of black bird, maybe a raven, cawed overhead as if telling the snake, "She's over here." The ground turned from grass to rock. Her rubber soled shoes padded loudly. God, she wanted to tell her feet and the damn bird to shut up.

Flickering light came from inside the rock formation she understood now to be an entrance. She prayed no demons greeted her. The closer she came to the mouth of the pyramid, the smoother the ground became, like glass, and reflected firelight off the surface.

Slosh. Slosh. Slosh.

Her feet hit a thin layer of water. Kalani slowed but didn't stop. The ground was like stiff pudding under her feet, and if she stopped moving, she'd sink. She stumbled when she struck solid rock again, but caught herself before face-planting. Glancing over her shoulder, Kalani discovered the snake had not followed her through the quicksand.

The gap into the pyramid glowed orange and yellow, and a fire blazed just inside. Nothing lingered near the entryway. The raven had flown off somewhere. She crept inside. The deeper she went, the dimmer the light became.

A piercing scream echoed from down a pitch-black tunnel on her left. The path straight in front of her looked more promising, yet her instincts told her to go left instead. Another scream shot toward Kalani. Her heart beat faster, vibrating her chest. She stayed close to the wall, using it as a guide as the passageway grew darker. Humidity filled the air, compromising her lungs. A pungent odor smacked her in the face and her eyes watered. A cross between horrible BO and rotting meat. Was there anything worse? She plugged her nose and breathed through her mouth.

Kalani reached the end of the last bit of light. She couldn't see anything. Her hands itched. Sucking in a breath, she rubbed her palms together. The itching traveled up her arms to her elbows.

What the what...is this?

She pressed her lips into a thin line to keep from whimpering. Damn, why had she come alone? If she made it out alive without losing her sanity, she'd beg Dru for forgiveness and happily spend the rest of her life with him.

Something clutched her shoulder, she wrenched away, and wheeled around punching, elbows first. Whatever had her, a demon or something else, grunted. Heat radiated off its body, which was the only reason she knew where the creature was. The smell masked any scent it carried. Kalani blindly threw punches, some connecting. But enough of them that the creature went down and stayed down. Her knuckles stung.

She found the wall on her left side and continued further into the passageway. As she went along, some areas of the wall had soft spots. Another wordless screech resounded, this one familiar. Was it Jade? Could it be that easy to find her? Kalani had only encountered three beings so far, the snake, a raven, and the likely demon whom she had nearly effortlessly taken down.

Kalani ran toward the terrified voice. Jade's voice. However, she didn't dare call her name. The wall of the passageway curved to the left. Shadows danced in the light shining on the rock on the opposite side. The silhouettes looked like hunchbacked creatures with a row of spikes down their spines. She'd never met a demon resembling this.

The wall on her left ended. Keeping low to the ground, she peered around the sharp curve. A fire burned in a pit dug into the middle of a circular room. The flames shot up, snapping and tossing embers into the air. Four large iron cages hung at various heights from the ceiling around the bonfire. Two were empty. A teal-haired woman sat slumped with her head hanging forward, chin pressed to her chest in the one closest to Kalani. In the last cage, and the furthest away...naturally, Jade sat hunched over on her knees, her face in her hands.

Kalani looked around for demons.

The itching sensation returned. This time she looked at her hands and screamed.

* * *

Dru

Johnson Park was deserted this time of night. Humans generally stayed indoors after nine o'clock. Demons mostly came out at night. So unless a demon sought a different life separate from their Collective, they returned home before sunrise.

"How do we find the portal? And are we sure this is a good idea?" Riordan asked Dru.

"Look for something not right. And no, this is *never* a good idea." He walked past the play structure, exploring all the sides. Out of the corner of his eye, a single swing swayed despite the surrounding ones not moving. "Get over here, I think I found something."

"Oh, great," Riordan remarked sarcastically. He dropped a handful of woodchips and came over.

"What did you expect to find in a pile of woodchips?"

"Shut up," Riordan snorted.

"Come on," Dru said, indicating Riordan follow him.

"Oh, boy."

Dru stopped. "You don't have to come, you know." The pull of the portal ruffled his hair. They were close.

"Like I'm going to let you die all by yourself. What kind of friend would I be?"

"Alive."

"Eh, breathing is overrated anyway."

Dru shook his head. "No. It's really not."

Tracking further away from the swing set, their clothes and hair pulled forward. Without thinking, Dru dug his heels into the grass. Riordan did the same. "Whoa!" They both lost their footing and fell, smacking the ground. Dru bit his tongue. From the grunts Riordan made, he had too.

A powerful force dragged them feet-first toward the unseen gateway. Dru clawed the dirt, frantically scratching deep grooves in the earth. The soles of his Nikes met with a hard invisible barrier. His body lifted off the ground vertically and slammed into it face first. "Ahhh! Fu—" He bounced off the barrier, landing in a heap next to Riordan, who rolled on the ground writhing in pain as he tried catching his breath. The strong pulling force ceased.

Riordan finally drew in a full breath. "What the fuck was that?"

"Like I know," Dru spat, getting to his knees.

"Do you think the portal moved on us?"

"Either that or closed on us."

Kalani's scent lingered in the air. She had gone through the portal.

CHAPTER ELEVEN

Kalani gripped her wrist and examined her hand. "Oh God. Oh my God. No!" Her fingers and hand up to her wrists had turned black. Three rows of tiny spikes similar to rose thorns covered the backs of her hands. Her skin continued blackening, the color creeping up her arms. She had to get out of this place before she looked like one of those creature's shadows she saw on the wall.

Something moved in her peripheral and she snapped her head to the right. Kalani tried screaming again, but only air eked out. Standing five feet away with its head cocked to the side was one of the creatures in the flesh. Not a shadow. Its skin pitch-black. Light from the fire created just enough contrast that she could see its confused expression. As if also wondering why her skin had changed color.

It stepped closer toward her. Now she knew the creature was male. Kalani stayed crouched against the wall. He lunged forward and squatted with his face inches from hers.

Please don't kill me.

She squeezed her eyes shut then opened them slowly. His irises were purple. "Oh, fuck," she whispered, not realizing she said it out loud until he recoiled. Was this how demons appeared in their home realm? Barbs covered the demon's hands too. He leaned even closer to her face and inhaled. Kalani pulled her head back. He went in closer. A round medallion hanging around his neck swung. She shivered from his cool breath.

"That's no way to ask a lady out on a date," she said, refusing to show fear.

He backed away, hissing. When he reached

the wall, the rock swallowed him, leaving only his eyes showing. How did that work? Had he been swallowed or...was the wall not made of rock like she thought? She remembered the softer spots along the wall and shuddered. Kalani squinted into the dim lighting. The eyes disappeared.

A metal on metal squealing brought her attention toward the cages. Two spike-backed creatures with vicious looking canine-like faces yanked the unconscious teal-haired woman out of her cage by the ankles. Her back and head hit the ground with a sickening thud. The woman didn't react—no crying, no voluntary movement at all. Kalani glanced away. Was she dead?

Kalani waited until the demons left the room with the woman. She cursed herself for not going over there and saving her, but more than likely it would be pointless, and only get her killed. Realizing she didn't have much time, she ran for Jade's cage.

"Jade," she whispered. "Jade." The bottom of the cage was over her head. Jumping in the air, Kalani grabbed two of the vertical bars with her hands. Jade gasped and before Kalani could pull herself up, her best friend scooted to the opposite side of the cage. With Kalani being the lighter of them, the iron prison tilted, causing her to slip down so all Jade saw was two tar black hands clinging to the bars. Her feet dangled above the ground.

"Get away from me." Jade's dismissive tone lacked emotion. She said those words like she'd already given up hope of survival.

Kalani's heart pinched. "No, it's me."

"Get away—Kalani?"

"Come to this side. Where the door is."

The cage shifted again as Jade moved. Kalani worked herself over to the door one bar at a time. Her friend's face was covered in grime and her clothes were torn. Her bloody knees showed through her ripped jeans and her shirt had a slash across the chest. What had been done to her? She'd ask how Jade was but there was no time.

Kalani yanked on the door with one hand, it didn't budge even though it wasn't padlocked or chained. She maneuvered so both hands gripped the bars on the door and she set her feet below on the bottom rim of the cage.

Throwing her weight backward, Kalani yanked with every ounce of muscle and power she possessed. Metal snapped and one of the bars broke off. Kalani tossed the rod aside.

Jade tried squeezing through the gap but she couldn't fit. If Kalani cracked off one more piece her friend could escape. She leaned back with a hard jerk as Jade pushed from the inside. Instead of breaking another bar, the door flew open, sending Kalani to the ground. Jade landed on top of her.

"Ooph!"

"Are you o—"

"We don't have time, let's go." Kalani rolled her off and jumped to her feet.

"You came."

Kalani grasped Jade's hand, pulling her up. "Of course, now run." What was with the chit-chat? Didn't she know this was a rescue mission? They sprinted toward the passageway where the demon had melded into the wall. Several sets of eyes popped open. Jade screamed.

"They're harmless."

I hope.

Behind them, hissing sounds began. The volume increased and Kalani glanced over her shoulder. Creatures like the one that had hissed and retreated into the rock stepped away from the walls on both sides of the tunnel.

"Oh, shiiit!"

Kalani raced forward faster but Jade had trouble keeping the pace and stumbled. She took her friend's hand, nearly dragging her along.

The demons chased them down the tunnel, some crawling along the ceiling and others emerging from the stone walls in their wake.

Fuck this!

Kalani stopped. The demons closed in on them.

"W-what are you doing?" Jade yelled.

"Hold still!" Kalani wrapped her arms around her friend. Although it was possible, she had never attempted what she was about to do.

"Whatever you're thinking, do it now," Jade said.

"Hold on to me."

One of the creatures clutched Kalani's shoulder. She drew in a deep breath and willed her body to vaporize.

"What's happening—!" Jade hollered in her ear.

Kalani pictured them flying out of the pyramid, over the quicksand and rock. Across the grass with the snake and...

"Ahhhhh!" Jade was still yelling as they reformed outside...right on the quicksand pond. The demon who had Kalani's shoulder had made the trip with them. He turned out to be the same one that had hissed in her face, with the necklace.

Luckily, Kalani understood they weren't where she'd intended they end up. She quickly moved across the sands of death while the demon struggled.

Where's Jade?

"Help!"

Shit.

Kalani pivoted and found Jade waving her hands. The sands engulfed her up to her knees.

"Stay calm." Man, her energy was going to be greatly depleted after this. Kalani vaped to her, said, "Hug me," and vaped again with Jade in a bear hug. This time they made it to solid ground. She hadn't noticed before, but a liquid barrier stretched forever in both directions and above to infinity on the other side of the grass where she had landed in this wretched place. "Whatever you do, don't stop running."

"Why?"

"Head for the barrier."

"What?"

"Just head straight and keep going. Don't stop for anything."

"But there's a—"

"I know. Go through it. It's fine."

The sand covered demon sprinted toward them. Jade yelped.

"Go. Now! I'm right behind you!" Kalani screamed.

CHAPTER TWELVE

KALANI

Kalani squared off with the demon, her hands curled into fists. "I told you, ask politely if you want a date." Fighting him out in the open, with the portal right behind her, lessened the fear she had in the pyramid. Vaping with Jade hadn't drained her as much as she imagined. Here, power seemed to seep into her veins from the air itself.

The ebony skinned demon cocked his head like he didn't understand the word 'date' or maybe any of the words.

"I'll tell you what, let's just be friends."

He charged Kalani, running so fast she couldn't track his legs.

Jade better be sprinting for the gateway, she thought.

No way was the demon truly after a Bator over a human. But this demon had to go through Kalani first.

She launched herself into the air, rising twenty feet off the ground, a war cry leaving her throat. Only in the dim recesses of her mind was she even aware of making the sound. The demon jumped to meet her but only managed a few feet in the air. Kalani came down on the bastard, her fist connecting with his head. He grabbed her around the waist. They hit the grass and log-rolled several yards entwined together.

The demon wound up on top. He punched her in the face, the barbs on his fingers leaving a pattern of cuts in her flesh. Her fangs descended as she dodged another jab. His fist hit the ground beside her head.

A small window of retaliation opened as the demon's face came closer. Kalani rolled up and head butted him in the face. He grunted, purple phosphorescent blood bursting from his nose.

She shoved him to his back by the shoulders, straddled his hips, and pummeled his face, head, neck, everywhere she could. But dammit, he stayed conscious throughout the beating.

Frustrated and uncertain of what would happen if she left him alive, she did what any true Bator might do in this situation. Okay, okay, she only thought about one Bator though. Beautiful, sexy, pain in the ass Dru. Of course, he could have said the same of her.

Peeling her lips off her elongated canines, Kalani sunk her fangs into the front of his neck and tore out a section of his windpipe. She spat it out before her gag reflex kicked in.

The demon clutched his throat with both hands, blood spurting between his fingers. His mouth opened while he tried breathing. She almost pitied him. "Turns out we'll *not* be friends." He fell still and his head lolled to the side, his body disintegrating into ash. "And I'll be taking this," she said, grabbing the medallion and shaking it free of demon dust. Kalani examined the markings then shoved the piece into her front pocket.

She stood and brushed off her pants, wiped her mouth with the back of her hand. "Ew...yuk." When she straightened and looked up, an army of ebony, spiny demon creatures was heading toward her. And she'd just killed one of their own.

Behind her, Jade screamed.

Why the hell hadn't she left yet? Kalani ran at her friend, who walked backward into the barrier. But not through it. The gateway looked like the murky surface of a lake on the vertical. It rippled around her.

Kalani stuck her hands out, shoving Jade through.

* * *

Dru

Dru sat on one of the swings next to Riordan. He kicked at the woodchips. "What the fuck man, do we wait here?"

Riordan didn't answer. A response wasn't necessary; they were both worried about Kalani. Silence hung in the air for a few minutes. Dru rubbed his palms on his thighs. Jumped up and paced in front of the swings. "I can't stand this. We should be doing something."

Riordan glanced at him. "Sun's coming up."

The air warped and a circle of wavy liquid appeared above the ground. Something pushed against the barrier from the other side. A form shaped like a person, but covered with the watery substance. The barrier stretched then Kalani and

Jade crashed to the ground at Dru's feet. Clear liquid splashed down around the them. The women scampered away from where they landed.

The skin on Lani's arms was black and thorny. The color faded, though. "We're not alone!" she shouted.

Dru and Riordan leapt into battle stances, unsheathing daggers. Bullets wouldn't stop a demon, or any creature from a Collective's realm. Their throats had to be slit or ripped out; every other wound healed. Except for a beheading. Entire limbs even grew back.

Three disgusting spiny demons burst into this realm. With his two daggers, Riordan sliced off the head of the nearest onyx-colored creature. Glowing purple blood spurted everywhere. Some sprayed into Dru's face and mouth. The body and head crumbled into ash.

Shaking that shit off, Dru tackled a demon. He wrapped his arms around its neck, cranking the head around and...*crunch*. The neck broke and he let the head fall, face up. Before the bastard had a chance to heal, Kalani severed his carotids with the blade Riordan tossed at her.

Another demon held a limp Jade under his arm like a rag doll. This idiot had demon blood on his hands. "Set her down!" Dru demanded.

"I don't think they understand English," Kalani said.

"You really weren't paying attention during training, were you?" Even though this wasn't the time for this argument, Riordan understood it was a distraction. He sneaked around behind the demon and lopped his head off. Dru lunged for Jade, catching her before she hit the ground.

On Dru's right, a wide hole in the barrier opened. An army of demons moved toward the gaping expanse. However, they stopped when reaching the portal and stayed on their side.

Rays of sunshine peeked through the trees surrounding the park. Fortunately, from the looks of the demons, they'd been in the passageways so long they'd transformed into Spines. It would take weeks before they would return to normal and be able to withstand sunlight. What had Kalani done to provoke what appeared to be an entire Collective? The long gash in the barrier closed, shutting off their snarling.

"All right, what did you do?" Dru asked Kalani.

"Nothing."

"Uh huh, right. How come your chin's glowing? You wouldn't have happened to take out their leader, did you?" Dru gently laid Jade on the grass, kneeling by her side.

"They all look the same." Kalani came over and

took her friend's hand, pressing the back of it to her cheek.

Dru took a deep breath, dragging his hands down his face. "Now I know you weren't paying attention."

"They look the same, what do you mean did I take out their leader? They are a collective, how do they have leaders?"

"They do. The leader would be the one that told them to move."

"They don't speak."

"Couldn't you hear them in your head?"

"It was noisy. Yes, but..."

Dru laughed without humor. "Their leader always wears a gold medallion. Would've been part of the pyramid walls. He can leave the walls, but the others can't without his permission."

She formed an "O" with her mouth. "Oh."

"Yeah, oh. Did the one you killed happen to have a medallion around his neck?"

"Maybe. But doesn't that mean they won't do anything without—"

Dru scrubbed his face with his hands. "You can't be serious. There's a hierarchy they follow and the new leader will seek revenge. It's what they do."

"Great. Fabulous. Tremendous. Lovely."

"Yeah, you're pretty much fucked," Riordan said.

"Can we discuss how fucked I am later?" Kalani snapped. Jade needs medical attention right now."

Chapter Thirteen

KALANI

The ambulance had arrived ten minutes after Riordan explained over the phone to Cutler what happened. Dru and Riordan vaped to the hospital while Kalani rode with Jade.

An IV tube ran from Jade's vein to a bag of saline. She'd been extremely dehydrated from all the blood loss from her time in the Collective realm.

The paramedic checked her pupils for the third time. Yep, they were still fixed, but apparently not fixed and dilated. She was breathing on her own, and her pulse was fine considering. But her eyes stared blankly and she hadn't uttered a single word, only lay there strapped to the gurney, blinking occasionally.

Jade was catatonic.

Tears stung Kalani's eyes. Her friend seemed fine inside the other realm. Within minutes of being back on Earth, her mind shut down, leaving Jade a shell. What was this sickness that place brought on humans? No doctor had figured it out.

"What's going to happen to her?" she asked the paramedic.

"Not up to me," he said. He possessed a certain compassion that only made Kalani cry more.

"You know, don't you, what happens in these cases?" She sniffed.

"ICU for observation then state psych ward unless her family takes—"

"I'm all she's got." Her parents were elderly, they couldn't possibly take care of her. Kalani would call them, though.

A surprised expression came over his face. He shrugged. "Then you should take her, those state facilities are..."

Scary.

She refused to hear anymore and tuned out the paramedic. She couldn't even think about leaving her best friend in a mental hospital. However, Kalani didn't have the means to care for Jade or the money for a full-time at-home caregiver.

For the rest of the ride, Kalani sat mutely, tears rolling down her cheeks.

The brakes squealed as the ambulance stopped on the circular driveway in front of the sliding emergency room doors. Medical personnel rushed out to greet Jade and wheeled her away.

The ambulance driver patted Kalani on the shoulder. "This probably doesn't mean much, but thank you for your service."

Service?

"Oh, I'm not..." she shook her head. "I just...she's my friend."

"I know, I could tell. Never seen a Bator cry over one of us before."

Kalani thought of protesting, denying her species. "There's no need for name calling," she muttered under her breath. Bator was a term she loathed. Their species had a name and that wasn't it. Osiris Hominum Daemonium or Homodae, for short.

"What was that?"

"Homodae. We're Homodae."

"My apologies. Let's go see about your friend."

* * *

Dru

Dru and Riordan sat in the ER waiting room. Dru chuckled to himself. When they had arrived, several humans vacated their seats and stood on the other side of the room. Although, he wondered if it had more to do with him being shirtless and covered in demon blood than his DNA.

A couple of nurses and a doctor rushed past them and through the entrance doors. Seconds later, they burst back inside wheeling Jade into the ER. Dru leapt to his feet and trotted to the glass doors. Kalani walked toward him with the ambulance driver, who nodded.

As the doors slid open, she wiped tears from her eyes. Dru held his arms out for her. She stepped into him, but the embrace only lasted a moment. "We need to find Jade."

Dru reached for her hand but she ignored the gesture. The slight may not have been intentional, although it wounded him. He told himself to stop being a baby and suck it up. She'd never made any promises to him. So they had sex. Big deal.

Like an obedient Bator, he followed her to the triage station. A nurse told Kalani they could go see

Jade and showed them the way. Riordan stayed in the waiting room.

Jade lay in a seated position on the hospital bed with her eyes open, staring straight ahead.

"She's got the sickness," Dru said dumbly.

"I know," Kalani said. She held Jade's hand. "Wake up, you're safe now." Ha! Wasn't that a load of crap? "Squeeze my hand if you can hear me. Come on, please." Jade's eyes moved a tad in Kalani's direction then went right back to staring at nothing.

After an hour of watching Jade stare, she was moved to the ICU for observation. A doctor asked them to leave.

CHAPTER FOURTEEN

KALANI

They reached as far as some benches outside the hospital near the ER before Kalani broke down. She needed a minute and parked her bottom on the cement seat, covering her face with her hands. Everything sucked. Her best friend was catatonic, and now an entire Collective wanted her dead. The only good thing about recent events was Dru coming back into her life. Even though she had gone to Bator Tower for Jade's sake, she'd found love too. How crazy was that?

Kalani missed Dru so much. If she were honest with herself, their bond began when they were teenagers. She loved him. Too bad she'd screwed up her chances for a happily ever after. It's hard to love someone when you're dead.

Riordan whistled. "Kalani?"

"Huh?" She glanced up.

"Just wondered if you were still with us. We should get back home."

"I'm so screwed, aren't I?"

"Not necessarily," Dru said.

"How is she not royally screwed?" Riordan asked Dru, running a finger over the turquoise beads at his throat and spinning them around the black braided cord. Kalani kept her eyes on his neck. She had taken Red from him without asking. Probably hurting him too by using him. Tricking him. Gawd... Why the hell was she thinking about this now? Oh, yeah, penance before death.

"Well for starters, they aren't interested in starting a war," Dru said.

War? Who said anything about war? What are they talking about?

She needed to pay attention but her guilt kept

her wrapped inside her own head. Riordan was a good Bator.

"I'm sorry," she blurted.

"You don't need to apologize," Dru answered.

She got up, glided toward Riordan, and stood in front of him, allowing ample personal space if he wanted her away from him. "I'm sorry, I...I shouldn't've tricked you into thinking..."

Riordan smiled. "You did what you had to. I get it."

"Do you?"

Dru looked cross at Riordan. He put his arm around her waist, his wide palm warming her body. Kalani let her...*mate* show his claim on her. And what do you know, she loved it. She placed her hands over his.

Kalani sighed. "What can we do about Jade?"

"I've been thinking about that. I may have a solution, or at least a temporary one," Dru said.

"Why do I have a feeling I'm not going to like this?"

"You need a place for Jade to get the care she needs and Cutler would love to have you back. Why not a trade?"

"What are you saying? I definitely don't like where this is headed."

"Our medical staff is the best, why not take her to headquarters?"

"And?"

"And you come back to the Patrol Guard. I like it." Cutler's deep voice cut the humid air.

Where the hell had he come from? He annoyed her already and she hadn't even formally met the director, or agreed to anything.

"It's settled, then. I'll arrange for her transport," Cutler said decisively. "We have a nice medical suite for her."

"Her name is Jade. I don't remember agree—"

"You really don't have a choice, dear. People go to prison for the things you've done."

"What things?" Okay, yeah, she had committed breaking and entering. "Sorry about the Red."

"I wasn't referring to you destroying the Dispensary."

"I didn't destroy it. It was one cooler."

"Entering a Collective is illegal. In addition, you almost caused my two best guards to break the law for you."

"That's illegal? Since when?"

Cutler's forehead crinkled.

"She didn't pay attention in class," Dru explained.

"Ah. Well, catch her up then." Cutler walked into the hospital and disappeared around a corner.

"What just happened?" Kalani asked.

Dru smiled. "Looks like you have a new job, and a place for Jade to get the best round the clock care."

"I guess." She sighed with resolve. What choice did she have? She would do anything for Jade. And *maybe* she enjoyed killing demons more than she thought.

"There's an empty apartment across from mine I'm sure you can have."

"Across the hall, huh?"

Chapter Fifteen

KALANI

The strangest thing about the sickness was that Jade hadn't lost the ability to eat or sip water through a straw. The problem was someone had to feed her or hold the cup. She also didn't care whether she ate.

Kalani sat at Jade's bedside down in the Patrol Guard medical facility all day. Nothing had changed.

A few hours ago, her friend had sighed heavily, which had her hopeful for a fleeting moment.

The head of the medical staff, Dr. Bowman, entered the room without knocking. He studied his iPad, swiping a finger up the screen. "How's our patient?"

"Same," Kalani said.

"We'll start some therapy treatments tomorrow," the doctor told her while keeping his eyes on the electronic device. "I think it's important we keep her as mobile as possible."

Kalani nodded. Collective sickness didn't affect a person's ability to walk with assistance. "What do you think her chances are?"

"No one has ever recovered, but that doesn't mean she can't be the first."

"Thank you for saying so, even if you don't believe it." Kalani squeezed Jade's hand. The gesture wasn't acknowledged, not that she expected it would be.

Kalani sensed Dru's presence in the hallway outside the medical suite. He knocked softly. The doctor opened the door, nodded at him, and left her and Dru alone with Jade.

Dru placed his hands on Kalani's shoulders. "I'm worried about you."

"I wish there was something I could do for her."

"You got her out. Believe me, it's better than leaving her there."

"Is it? She's trapped in her own mind here."

"She's alive, and that's more than most get. At least she has a chance to get better here."

"Are you always this naïvely optimistic?"

"Why aren't you? Come upstairs with me. If anything changes, they've been instructed to inform you right away."

Kalani rose from the chair. He wrapped his arms around her. She sagged into him, pressing her forehead to his chest. "Can you give me a minute? I'll meet you upstairs."

"Don't be too long." He regarded Jade for a moment before leaving the room.

Kalani sat on the edge of the bed and pulled the pendant she'd stolen from the Collective leader from her pocket. She hadn't let it out of her sight, even carried it in the shower with her. The symbol on the round face was puzzling—the crook and flail representing Osiris. Why would the leader of a Collective wear such a thing? What did it mean? Questions for which she intended to find answers. Now wasn't the time, though.

She put the necklace away and spoke to Jade like she could respond. And who knew? Her friend might be entirely aware of her surroundings just unable to communicate for some reason. "What do you think of Dru? Hot, huh? I know you didn't get a good look at him, but trust me." Kalani smiled lopsidedly. "Hopefully you'll get to meet him soon. I love him. But don't tell him that. He'll get a big head. I'll come see you tomorrow so we can talk, okay?"

Jade blinked twice, yet her eyes remained unfocused at some distant point.

"I swear, if you're faking..." Oh, God, how she wished that was true, and tomorrow Kalani would come down here and they'd have a good laugh together. This sickness was like some sort of trance. "Well," she leaned over and kissed Jade's brow, "try and get some rest."

Kalani gave her friend one last look before going upstairs. Dru met her in the hallway outside his apartment. "Hey, you."

"Hi."

He went to the door across the way and opened it. "After you." She purposely brushed up against his chest as she entered the apartment. He tensed like she was rejecting him, which was completely ridiculous. Didn't he understand how she felt?

The apartment was larger than his, with a separate bedroom off a sitting area with a couch and a flat screen TV. She wandered through the rooms. "I don't like it."

"Why? You can decorate however—"

"That's not it, it's empty."

"You can add more furniture, make it yours."

She stopped in front of him. "That won't help. It'll still suck."

Dru chuckled. "I know. Well it's either this or wait for the Collective to find you at your human residence."

"That's going to happen anyway, isn't it?"

Dru pursed his lips, shrugging. "They won't all come for you at once. They will send scouts."

"That's really not all that comforting."

"Wasn't supposed to be."

She pushed his shoulder. "I get it, I'm safer here than anywhere else."

"The Bator Cutler sent to get the things you requested from your home should be back soon. So do you want this apartment or look at another one?"

"Another one will be as sucky as this one."

"Sorry. They all suck," he laughed.

"Not yours."

"Yeah...no, it's horrible too."

"No. It's not."

"It's spartan, I've been meaning to decorate..."

She put her arms around his neck. "Shhh...it's the best."

"If you say so."

"I do. You know why it's the best?"

"Not a clue." He nuzzled her neck and she giggled.

"Because you're in it."

"Not right now, I'm not."

"Smart-ass."

"I try hard."

Kalani tilted her head back and laughed. "Yes, you do."

"I give up, why is mine the best?"

"You don't know?"

"Haven't we been through this?"

Kalani took his hand and led him back across the hall and into his apartment. She slammed the door shut. "I love this apartment. All the others lack one essential thing."

He grinned. "I can't imagine what."

"You."

Clutching his chest, he staggered backward.

"Stop playing, I'm serious."

"You love me, don't you?"

"Shut up. Yes. I love you. Dammit."

* * *

Dru

Dru smiled, his fangs dropping. Hearing those

words was an aphrodisiac like no other. He wanted her. Now.

"Are you saying you want to live with me?"

"No."

"You're a terrible liar. Before you move in here, there's something I need you to do for me first."

"First what? That implies there is a second thing involved?"

"Yeah. We're having sex."

"Do we have to?"

"Oh, you're going to enjoy what I do to you."

"So sure, are we?" She arched an eyebrow.

Pretending to ignore her snarky comment, he growled quietly. Her strength only further spurred his libido. "I didn't hear you complain before."

"I must've forgotten to."

He smirked and crooked his finger at her. "I'm going to pretend I didn't hear that."

"What, you want this?" She pulled down one strap of her tank top.

"Uh uh. Not yet." He removed his shirt.

"Why are you getting undressed then?"

"Can't I get comfortable?" he said, shucking his shoes and jeans.

"Any more comfortable and you'll be naked."

Dru teased the waistband of his boxer briefs. She eyed his hands. "What, you want this?"

A guttural growl pumped out of her. "Uh uh. Not—"

"You're so full of it. You've got a growl that says you do."

Kalani's lips parted as she eyed his manly bulge. A look passed over her face that he recognized immediately. She stepped closer to him, hopping on one foot then the other as she removed her shorts. Next, she peeled her sleeveless shirt off. Apart from her lacy panties, she was nude.

He grasped her wrist as she reached a hand toward his cheek and put it behind her back. "Not yet. I was serious."

She frowned, sticking out her lower lip and peering up through her lashes.

"You think that's going to work on me? Pouty face." It was working. His self-control waned.

"What was that something you wanted first?"

"Uh uh, no you don't, you're not turning this around on me." But she was. Quickly. "I want you to taste me first," he breathed, barely above a whisper.

"What was that?"

With short loud roar, he grabbed her ass with both hands, picking her up. He was done talking. She gasped and wrapped her legs around his hips. Her lips grazed his neck. She nipped his skin. Now he was gasping. "Taste me, Lani."

Kalani whispered softly in his ear, "We're both done for, you know."

"Promise me that's true." He'd dreamed of her coming back to the program. Not to be with him necessarily, but so she would be in his life again. Even if that meant she shared her bed with another. He'd hate it. But he loved her enough to let her find happiness with whomever she chose.

"I promise."

He ran his hand up the nape of her slender neck. She purred, then struck his vein. "Uh...oh." Dru could no longer tell if they were standing, sitting, or lying down. Everything disappeared. The world fell away. With love in their hearts, the taking of Red meant so much more, it was a vow which signified their bond. Their unbreakable union.

Holding her to his chest, he laid her on the bed. She released his vein, the punctures healing themselves. He shredded her panties and tossed the scraps over his shoulder.

She flipped them over and straddled him. "Hmm, we have a problem."

"No, *we* don't."

"Your boxers are in the way." She rocked her hips. He groaned, biting his bottom lip. His hands caressed the swells of her breasts, his thumbs passing over the rosy tips. Her head tilted back and she moaned.

Ripping a gaping hole in his Hanes he said, "Not anymore." He sat up and bit the side of her neck. Red flowed into his mouth with a rush so fantastic it washed over his entire body. He'd still take from the supply of blood downstairs as needed. They would both require replenishment from another source every so often. But her blood, oh gods, no other tasted this unbelievable.

She whimpered when he readjusted his seal on her throat.

"Did I hurt you?" he asked.

"No. I want to feel you inside me."

Dru shuddered, his muscles tensing. "I want to be inside you too."

* * *

Kalani

Yasssss. Bator sex again. She couldn't wait any longer. Kalani loved the feel of his bare skin pressing against hers. His thick muscled arms wrapped around her, making her feel safe, despite the Collective army wanting her dead. Most likely torturing her first. She should be frightened, scared, something, but she wasn't. Not now.

Dru laid his back on the mattress with his hands behind his head, his sculpted chest and abs on full display. Dang, he was sexy as hell. Fire burned in his eyes, half-masted and glowing like hot coals.

"Thought you wanted me inside you?" he asked.

"And I thought you were going to do things to my body."

"I was bluffing." He smiled with a devilish grin. "Do whatever you want to me. I'm yours."

As if her heart didn't surge with those two words. *I'm yours.* "In that case..." Kalani rubbed herself on the underside of him. His head pitched back. She rose to her knees, taking him inside her. "I'm yours too."

"I love you," he said breathlessly.

"Ah, dammit, I love you too. Let's hope I survive. I killed their *leader.*"

Oh, God, please let me survive...

She leaned down and kissed his velvety lips.

"You will. With my last breath, you will."

They took turns making love to each other until neither one of them could stay awake.

Dru would love, protect, honor, and cherish her forever. Kalani knew down to her marrow that together they could conquer any obstacle, even a legion of demons out for vengeance. After all...they were gods.

PART TWO

STEALING NIGHT

CHAPTER ONE

RIORDAN

Riordan sat at Jade's bedside, reading aloud from the Official Bator Field Manual. She blinked occasionally, her breaths strong and steady despite the tiny bit of spit glistening in the corner of her mouth. Nobody was certain whether or not she was aware of her surroundings. She didn't appear to be listening either.

The door pushed open and Director Cutler stuck his head in the room. "What are you doing down here?"

"Doctor Bowman said we should talk to her. It might help bring her out of the trance. I think it's—"

"I know what the doctor said." Cutler stepped into the room. He glanced at Jade with a furrowed brow, his eyes lingering on her face. She stared straight ahead, never changing her expression. Was he attracted to the female? "I want you out on patrol with Kalani."

"She's ready to be on her own."

"I'm not as confident as you."

"Why don't you trust her?" No sooner had the words left his lips did he realize it wasn't a trust issue but a protective issue. Cutler wasn't in love with her, he wanted to make sure she came home alive to Dru at the end of a shift each night. Hunting demons was dangerous even though Bator were stronger and could vaporize out of a no-win situation if they needed to.

"This isn't about trust."

Oh, boy, here comes the lecture.

"There are strict training protocols," Cutler continued. "Every Bator goes through a rigorous training and she must complete the steps."

Kalani had dropped out of the training program ten years ago, returning only three months earlier.

However, she had fought and killed the leader of the demon Collective. By herself. This now meant she had an entire legion wanting to spill her blood and dance on her entrails. But hey, nothing to worry about. Yeah right. On second thought, she should have the entire Patrol Guard with her at all times.

"Are you listening to me?" Cutler asked, clearly annoyed given his expression.

"Yeah."

"What did I say then?"

"To babysit Kalani until you're comfort—"

"And?"

"And that's it. Trick question."

Cutler snorted. "Get the hell out of here and go find her. She's probably on the roof."

Riordan thought about saying "no shit" but opted to keep his mouth shut. He left the room and took a right toward the elevators.

Kalani was right where the director had suggested he find her. Riordan let the roof access door slam shut, allowing her to know he was there. She stood close to the edge, the wind catching her black hair, lifting it off her shoulders. Her scent carried on the warm breeze. He inhaled deeply. "How's it going?" he asked, nudging her shoulder.

"Eh. Quiet." She gathered her hair and tied it up with a rubber band. Another breeze blew across the roof and the wisps of hair around her neck danced.

How pointless was his obsession with her? She wasn't going to dump Dru and suddenly fall into his bed. He fiddled with the hemp and turquoise bead necklace she had made for him ten years ago. He'd been a wide-eyed twelve-year-old with a stupid crush back then. Now? The crush made him pathetic.

"Are you okay?" she asked.

"Yeah, why?"

"You seem distracted."

"I'm sensing." Demon activity had been relatively minimal for the last a couple of months. But this didn't mean things were slowing down, rather they were organizing for a string of attacks or something on a larger scale. Riordan wondered if this would result in more human females being abducted than ever before. Or Kalani's assassination.

Far below them, a siren wailed. Riordan jumped onto a gargoyle and squatted, overlooking the city street. His leather pants creaked. Kalani peered over the edge of the building. Her upper body hung so far out, he worried that she might fall. "Kalani. Be caref—" He stopped himself from finishing the sentence.

She pulled back and smiled at him, shaking her head. "Relax." Kalani leaned forward again. "Woo. Oh, no, it's so high. I'm so scared."

He smiled crookedly, glaring at her. "Go ahead,

make fun of me, but you won't be laughing when you plunge to your death."

"Good gods. Dramatic much?"

Yeah, he was being dramatic, since Bator could vaporize, virtually eliminating the threat of death. Riordan shifted on the statue to get better footing. The muscles between his shoulder blades tingled. The sensation rose up the back of his neck, spreading a prickling warmth to the top of his head. He stood. "You feel that?" he whispered, keeping his eyes focused on the tiny cars zipping down the street.

He swiveled his head in her direction. The only thing occupying the space where she had been were black tendrils of mist. She had vaped.

Sonofa...

CHAPTER TWO

RIORDAN

Riordan dove off the roof. Man, she was going to get herself killed with her leap-before-thinking attitude. Or in this case vape-before-thinking. Fortunately, three months ago Kalani had taken Red from him, enabling him to track her. He turned himself into mist. A few seconds later, he landed in the middle of the freeway next to her. Cars whipped past them, kicking up road dust. A semi-truck flew by, stinging his face with tiny rocks.

Kalani stuck her hand straight out in front of her as if she could stop the speeding car heading for them with her mind. What the hell was she doing? Riordan grabbed and tugged her waist. She held steady, only swaying slightly on her feet.

"We're going to get hit!"

"They'll stop."

A loud horn blared. The car wasn't slowing down. A bus nearly blew Riordan off his feet. Kalani vaped and reformed, avoiding the tiny rocks that pelted him.

The car's brakes squealed. Riordan vaped to the vehicle's roof while she jumped onto the hood, looking like a crazed lunatic. The orange of her eyes flared. Her fangs descended. She peeled her upper lip back in a snarl. She was dangerous like this.

And sexy as hell.

He had no time to deal with his ridiculous *never-going-anywhere* crush right now. A demon that had been hanging off the back of the car from the rack flung himself onto Riordan. They hit the roof. Hard. Landing on his front forced the air from Riordan's lungs. The car skidded to a halt, sending them sliding forward into Kalani. "Watch out!"

She leapt over Riordan and the demon.

He hit the ground, his upper back and shoulders taking the brunt of the fall. Heat radiated from the front of the car. The wheels rolled forward, threatening to crush him. A fist slammed into his cheek, knocking his head into the asphalt road. Riordan bucked beneath the demon. The bastard grabbed Riordan's jacket up by the collar, pitched, and rolled them to the side away from the tires.

Riordan sacrificed his face to another punch. He slipped his hand around the hilt of his dagger, pulling the blade free from its sheath. He stabbed the demon in the neck then shoved the creature off him. Riordan vaped back onto the vehicle's roof. It swerved wildly over the white lines. Other vehicles swerved, narrowly missing them.

Kalani was inside, yelling at the driver. "The bastard's ash, stop the damn car!"

Riordan looked around. No other demons seemed to be around, nor could he sense any activity nearby. Usually, demons attacked motorists in packs of at least four. What the hell was going on? Something was off.

The driver finally brought the car to a stop on the shoulder. Riordan jumped down off the roof and got into the car. Behind the wheel with her forehead resting on the steering wheel was a teal haired woman. Obviously a dye job.

"Hey, don't I know you?" Kalani asked her.

The woman kept her head down, panting heavily, gripping the steering wheel tightly.

"Deep breaths." Kalani said.

"Need I remind you, staying here like this isn't the best of ideas?" Riordan asked. Kalani glanced at him with a scowl on her face. He narrowed his eyes. "At least get us off this damn highway."

Kalani huffed. She placed her hand on the woman's shoulder. Teal shrugged it off. "He's right. Unfortunately."

"Unfortunately? I'm hurt," he said sarcastically.

"Get over it," Kalani threw over her shoulder from the front seat. "What's your name?" she asked Teal.

"Nadine."

Riordan liked Teal better.

"Nadine, are you all right to drive?" Nadine nodded then switched to shaking her head. "Why don't you trade places with me then?"

"O-okay." The women swapped seats. Nadine slid over to the passenger seat while Kalani got out and went around to the driver's side. From his seat behind Kalani, Riordan stared at Nadine's profile. He traced the outline of her face, memorizing her features. A tear dripped off her chin. She swiped a hand under her eye then dried her fingers on her pants. He was curious what she thought about sitting there so quietly. Did she have a boyfriend?

Did she live alone? Was anyone warming her bed at night. And why did he care? What the hell was wrong with him? Disgusted with his stupid questions that were none of his business, he leaned back in his seat and crossed his arms.

Kalani drove them to the closest off ramp and stopped on a residential street.

"Where do you live?" Riordan asked the human female.

"Nowhere," Nadine said.

Kalani squinted in confusion. "Is that a street?"

Riordan snorted.

"What?" Kalani said.

"Oh, like that's the name of a street."

"It could be," Kalani said. "Why are you being an—"

"Is it a street?" he asked.

"Uh uh. I..." The woman wrung her hands in her lap.

"Do you have someplace safe to go?" Kalani asked.

"A friend's. You can take me there."

A friend? Boyfriend?

"What's the name of this *friend*?"

Kalani gave him a dirty look.

What? he mouthed.

"Quit being an ass," she whispered almost

inaudibly, but he understood perfectly what she said given her exaggerated mouth movements.

"Sam Woodson."

"We'll take you there," Kalani said.

"Is Sam a man or a woman?" he asked.

"Riordan, seriously? Knock it off. What difference does it make?"

"Just wanna know if she'll be safe there. That's what difference it makes."

"Uh huh. Right." She eyed him suspiciously. "I can handle this, you know."

"I know."

"Well, if you know, go home then. I got this."

"Fine." Riordan took a deep breath, inhaling Nadine's scent. Remembering it.

What am I doing?

He rolled down the window and vaped home.

CHAPTER THREE

RIORDAN

Riordan punched in the code on the keypad that had been installed after Kalani destroyed the Red Dispensary. Well, maybe not destroyed, but she had damaged two of the cooling racks looking to gain strength by ingesting copious quantities of blood. Dru had stopped her before getting her fill. She then fed from Riordan's vein after tricking him.

He may not have been tricked so much as wanting to believe she wanted him. Without thinking, Riordan brought his hand up to the black hemp necklace with three turquoise beads, Kalani had given him ten years ago. Back then the necklace was loose, now it was damn near a choker. He pushed the Dispensary door open.

Riordan opened the cooler rack door. Inhaling the coppery scent made his mouth water. His fangs descended. They had been half out and his cock half hard since his encounter with Nadine. What the what was wrong with him?

Palming three Red vials, he popped the corks and emptied the blood down his throat. He didn't bother tasting it. He took two more vials before closing the refrigerator.

"Hey, leave some for the rest of us," Dru said behind him.

"There's plenty. Jeez, can't a male get some Red without being hassled around here?"

"Who else has been hassling you? And chill out, man."

Riordan stepped into Dru's personal space. Dru puffed his chest, standing his ground and pushed a finger into Riordan's chest. "We having a problem?"

"No."

Dru tilted his head. "You sure? Because you seem to be having some sort of problem."

"Nope."

"You've been giving me shit since Kalani moved in. She isn't your—"

"I know she's not mine and never will be."

"All right. As long as you remember that."

"Why wouldn't I? I'm reminded every damn day by the way you look at each other." Honestly, Riordan was happy they had found love with each other. He cared enough about them both not to walk around acting jealous of Dru all the time. Envious, yes. But why? Did he want Kalani, or did he simply like the idea of being with someone? Okay, he did walk around jealous, looking for excuses to stay away from them. Especially, her.

* * *

Nadine

The girl Bator pulled along the curb in from of Sam's house. Nadine had no clue why she gave them Sam's name. She hadn't spoken to her ex in four years. He wasn't a friend. Even though she despised lying, she would do anything to save her sister.

"Do you want me to wait while you get inside?"

"No, that's all right. I have a key," Nadine told her. She bit her bottom lip. Was she going to live through this mess without a Bator killing her?

143

With all the lies, she'd have to keep a notebook to remember them. Being dishonest about Sam was going to be the first of many. Nadine tucked her hair behind her ears and let herself out of the mini-van.

The Bator chick got out, tossed her the car keys, and vaporized, leaving her alone. This hadn't been the plan, but the Bator seemed to know her for some reason, which was odd.

Nadine pivoted toward Sam's house. No lights were on inside.

Back in her van, she sat with the engine off. Her mind buzzed with whatever the demons had done to her. They kept her in a suspended cage in room over a fire pit. She didn't know how long they had imprisoned her. Demons would come for her, draining so much of her blood she'd pass out. God only knew what they did to her when she was unconscious. She would wake up with deep bruises all over her body. One day they forced her to drink blood until she puked. Told her they would set her and her sister Penny free if Nadine would do something for them.

A dark figure shadowed her window, blocking the porchlight from across the street. She gasped when there was a knock on the glass. Nadine twisted the key in the ignition. The engine wouldn't turn over.

Shit, take a deep breath.

"Teal," a familiar sounding man's voice said.

Teal? Oh, ha ha.

She turned on the dome light. The male Bator stood next the van. His fiery eyes glowed brighter for a moment, like they lit up when he saw her face. She rolled down the window. "How did you find me?" Never mind. She needed him.

"Tracked you."

"I'm s-sorry. How did you do that?"

And do I want to know?

"Sam Woodson. You gave us your *friend's* name, remember?" He said 'friend's' as if he was disgusted.

Yeah, I know the feeling, buddy.

"What are you doing here?"

"Might ask you the same question."

"Why is that?"

"You divorced this ass—guy four years ago."

"How do you," she swallowed hard, "know that?" What was with this Bator and why did he excite her? Her heart raced, and her cheeks warmed.

"I've got skills."

I bet you do with a body like that.

He smirked. Had she said that out loud?

"Why are you smiling?"

"I'm not."

"You smirked."

"That's not smiling. This is smiling." The corners of his mouth lifted, lips peeled from his teeth, and

145

long pointed canines eased down. Until tonight, Nadine had never been this close to a Bator.

"That's a grin, not a smile." She had an overwhelming urge for him to bite her. Sink his sharp pearly whites into her neck. She needed her head examined. "You look like the Cheshire cat, only more dangerous."

"Dangerous?" He chuckled under his breath. "You have no idea how much," he growled, sounding otherworldly. Dark. Sexy. Heat flooded her core.

"What do you want?" Her voice cracked and her mouth went dry.

"You know exactly what I want."

"Do I?" Nadine set her chin as if she was resisting him. She wasn't. Not even a little bit in her mind, but this wasn't the right time. Or the right place.

Quit lusting.

Taking a deep breath, she looked him in the eyes. Um, yeah, that wasn't a good idea. At. All.

"Oh, you do, it's all over your face."

"What's all over my face?"

"Lust."

"It is not." She cast her eyes downward. Why were they having this conversation? And why did she like it so much?

He disappeared in a fog of black smoke. She peered over the van's open window at the ground.

"What the hell?" Nadine knew Bator could turn to mist, but again, she had never seen it in person.

"Looking for me?" he drawled.

"Uh!" The male sat next to her, his face inches from hers, his breath warming her neck. "Get out of my car."

"This isn't your car. Any more lies you wish to tell?"

"What did you do, check on me?" She tried adjusting the heat in the car but remembered it wouldn't start.

"What lies? So I stole a car, are you going to arrest me?"

"I'm not a cop."

"You're Patrol Guard though. Don't you have some sort of authority?"

"Do you really think Bator would be given that kind of power? We're freaks of nature."

If he was a freak of nature, then what did that make her?

"Don't call yourself a freak," she spat. Why did his self-depreciation bother her? He pulled his head back and growled as if talking to himself, in an odd manner, reminding her of Chewbacca. "What was that?"

"I didn't say anything."

"You growled. Sounded like you were saying something."

"I wasn't."

"Sounded like it to—"

"Enough!" he shouted. "All right." Black mist swirled inside the car around their feet. He leaned in and whispered in her ear. "You're coming with me."

His arm came across her midsection. "Where are we goin—ahhhhhh!" The black mist became so dense around them she couldn't see anything.

CHAPTER FOUR

RIORDAN

Nadine was going to hate him for this if Cutler was wrong. Not that she wouldn't hate him anyway. Bring her in, the director had said. The Patrol Guard logged calls they went on which included adding details of the attack, including license plate numbers, and anything that seemed suspicious. The van was registered to a man who was killed during an attack where his wife had been abducted in the Rebelville District three days ago. The incident had been caught on someone's cell phone. The Demons took the car, which made no sense since they didn't steal cars. But how did Nadine wind up with it?

Riordan and Nadine reassembled on the Patrol Guard building's roof. Vaping with a non-Bator wasn't recommended. He felt fine though. Except, as soon as they became solid again, she passed out. He scooped her limp body into his arms and carried her inside.

The door at the bottom of the roof access stairs opened and Dru propped the door for him. "What's this?" he asked.

"Cutler wanted her brought in."

"I thought you didn't believe in the whole keep thy enemies closer?"

"Shut up."

Dru chuckled. "Yeah, Kalani told me."

"Told you what?"

"That you got really...excited about this one." He moved aside, allowing Riordan by with Nadine.

I did not. Did I? And Kalani noticed? Jesus.

Nadine's dangling wrist banged the door jamb. "Shit. Sorry."

"She can't hear you," Dru said.

Riordan sneered. "How do you know?"

"It's funny you know, you thought I acted crazy about Kalani and now you're eating your words."

"Oh, yeah, then why am I going to put her in the straps?" The "straps" room was in the second basement. He went to the bank of elevators and pressed the down button.

The doors slid wide, opening into a dark room. He walked across the empty room toward a door at the other end. Bator saw well in the dark. Riordan pressed his palm to the bio-scanner. The door creaked open. The room hadn't been used in a while. In the middle of the tiled expanse was a steel table with leather straps for someone's wrists, ankles, neck, and waist. He arranged Nadine on the table, splaying out her blue-green hair. The soft strands slipped through his fingers like silk. He hardened. Dru was right. Riordan was half crazed thinking about what he could do if she were awake and willing. He fastened the leather bindings around her wrists and ankles, leaving the neck and waist straps off.

Closing his eyes, he reached up and switched on the light above the table, turning his head from the brightness of the bulb until his eyes adjusted.

Nadine moaned. Her arms jerked, the restraints keeping them at her sides. She gasped and screamed.

"Calm down, Teal," he said.

"What did you do to me?"

"Relax. Nothing."

"What is this, a sex chamber? Lemme go!" Her face turned red as she struggled against the straps, screaming. She gave up after a few minutes. Either she had tired herself out or decided it was useless trying to squirm free.

The idea of the room being used for sex intrigued him. Although he would probably prefer being the one restrained. Which was...um, what had made him think that?

"This room is used for interrogations."

"This is illegal, you know."

"What's illegal?"

"Strapping someone to a table against their will."

Riordan smoothed back his hair. "Look, you put yourself here. I need answers and you're going to give them to me or you can stay strapped to this table forever."

"I'm not talking to you. I don't have any answers."

"How do you know? You don't even know what I was going to ask you."

She turned her voice into a bullhorn. He didn't know that was possible until now. He walked away from the table no longer able to tolerate the noise spewing from her mouth. Her voice cut out for a moment. "Where are you going?"

"You said you didn't have any answers, so I'm leaving."

"You're leaving me in here? For how long?"

"Forever." He placed his hand on the bio scanner. The lock released and he pushed open the door.

"Wait! I might have some answers."

"Too late." The door slammed shut behind Riordan. He didn't trust this female...woman, whatever she was. Kalani had recognized her from somewhere. Too many things were suspicious about Nadine's behavior. She was upset about being held captive but not as much as he would have expected.

Out in the anterior room, he pushed the button on the wall, opening the security camera console for the straps room. The cameras merely monitored what happened in the room, no sound was recorded. Nadine's body undulated, and her limbs pulled against the bindings. Her mouth was open, no doubt from screaming. The straps room was soundproof. Light from the bulb above her, made her seem like she had blonde roots. He brought the hand he'd used to touch her hair up to his face, taking a long breath.

"What are you doing, goofy?" Kalani stood in the doorway behind him.

He squeezed his eyes closed. "Do you need something?"

"Yeah. I remembered where I know her from. Although I don't think it'll matter to you."

"What wouldn't matter to me?"

"That's she's with them."

"With who?"

No.

He growled, catching Kalani's meaning. His eyes snapped toward the monitor. Nadine couldn't be a demon, could she? "She's not a demon!"

"Hey," Kalani put her palms up, "easy. I didn't say that, but she was in the place I found Jade. I thought she was dead honestly. They must've done something to her though, because why isn't she catatonic like Jade? Or any other human that's escaped a Collective."

He stared at the screen. Nadine's mouth stopped moving and her body stilled. Her chest heaved as if she was catching her breath. "Maybe they fed her their blood. Why is she here? What do you want?" He directed the last question to his prisoner.

"Why don't you ask her? But I think she's on a scouting mission for them."

"What do they think, we're stupid?"

Kalani smiled. "Well, she's here sooo..."

"Cutler's idea. Not mine."

"Come on, let's interrogate her together." She opened the straps room door and went inside without waiting for a response.

CHAPTER FIVE

NADINE

The female Bator from earlier charged into the room with the male lagging. Nadine glanced at her eyes. The red-orange glowed brightly. For a split second, a thread of envy passed through her heart. Nadine wished her eyes were at least something other than brown. Boring brown. Oh, that was absurd, why was she thinking about this now?

"So, Nadine, is it?" the female asked. "Where did you get the van?"

Demons gave it to me.

"I bought it."

The female smiled, but her expression wasn't genuine. "That's a lie."

"I'm not lying."

"You received stolen property from demons."

"What? No I didn't."

The female glared at her. "I see why Riory left you in here."

Nadine looked at him. That was his name? "Riory." Good Lord, why had she repeated his name?

His eyebrows knitted together. "Riordan," he said, in a low, growly tone. Their eyes met. She licked her lips and left her mouth open.

Damn.

He was hot. So hot she had to remind herself she was being held against her will. Why did she never want to leave though?

"I'm Nadine."

Shut. Up. He knows that.

"Yeah, and I'm Kalani. Now that we all know—"

Riordan purred loudly and stepped closer, his eyes roving over her body. She loved it. Nadine arched her back, imagining his mouth on her. She suspected he was doing the same.

Kalani tossed her hands up and smacked her thighs. "Are you two serious?"

Riordan grumbled under his breath, which sounded like a warning for Kalani to stay back.

"O-kay, have it your way, but I'm leaving before I become an accessory. You untie her, it's on you." Kalani may have left then, but Nadine wasn't paying close enough attention to her to know for sure.

Riordan's eyes glowed brighter like they had before he whisked her away from the van. Being in this vulnerable position should have frightened her, instead it made her crazy with lust. What was he going to do with her? Hmmm...what was he going to do? On second thought, maybe she should be scared. His lips parted. She couldn't tell if that was due to being rapt with sexual desire or out of necessity because his fangs had elongated, and he couldn't keep his mouth shut. "A-Are you g-going to drain my b-blood?" Her words caught in her throat.

"I'm not going to drain you, but I will bite you."

"Will it hurt?" When the demons drained her, they made slices in her wrists that healed after they licked the wounds. The cuts hurt a lot.

Leaning further over her, he placed a hand on her stomach. "It stings." She quivered. The leather straps creaked as she squirmed. His palm warmed her abdomen.

"Your hand is hot."

He slid his hand up between her breasts and she sucked in a breath. The anticipation of what he might do next made her hips surge off the table. Riordan glided his hand toward her belly and over one of her hips. She arched again and let out a gasp.

"Bite me," she whispered.

What was she saying? This was not the time to get caught up in some sexual fantasy, and with a Bator? It was one thing to fantasize, but this was real life, not some vampire novel. Humans had been told that Bator weren't nocturnal monsters since the first of their kind had been introduced to the world. However, true to humankind, many people feared them for no good reason. Nadine had never been afraid, she had been drawn to the species since childhood.

* * *

Riordan

What was he thinking? Riordan removed his hand from her body. This shit wasn't a good idea. At. All. She was lying to them about the van, which alone made no sense. Something was going on that he didn't understand. Well, two things were going on. One, Nadine was hiding something and two, he had never wanted anyone as much as her. He also didn't want to have her like this—strapped to a cold steel table at his mercy.

"Why did you stop?" she asked.

"I didn't want to."

"All right, then why did you?"

"I can't take advantage of you like this. It wouldn't be right."

"We both like each other."

He undid the straps on her wrists and ankles. "You're free to go. I'll get you out of the building. After that, you're on your own."

"You're letting me go?"

"You don't belong here, and whatever reason you have for driving that stolen van, I hope for your sake it wasn't a trick to gain our trust."

Her mouth dropped open. "A *trick*?"

"Don't think we're that stupid. Those demons tonight sacrificed their lives for you."

"What are you saying?"

"Teal, don't," he said, shaking his head. "I already know you were in a Collective. But what I can't figure out is why you are working for them."

She sat up and dangled her feet over the side of the table. Nadine didn't say anything for a few minutes as she stared at her hands in her lap. "They have my sister," she said softly. "They said they'd let us both go if I find some pendant for them."

Figured Cutler was right.

Dammit.

Riordan had hoped she'd deny the whole thing. Desperate people did desperate things. This was far from over. What was her next move? He couldn't let her leave now. "Thank you for telling me the truth. But now that I know what's going on I can't let you leave."

"But my sister. I have to help her."

"By being dead? That won't help her. You said they want some lost pendant."

"A Bator stole it from some important demon."

"Did they tell you who?"

"No. Just that it was most likely inside your headquarters."

Why didn't they tell her who stole the necklace? They knew it was Kalani, maybe not by name but certainly they could have described her face to Nadine. Why the stolen van ruse?

Shit.

Genius. The stolen van would seem suspicious and the director would want her brought in and interrogated. And here Riordan was believing the sob story about her sister. "Come with me," he said, heading for the door.

Her bare feet hit the floor and patted across the tile behind him. "Where are we going?"

"I want you to tell the director what's going on."

She stood so close to him on the elevator ride

up to Cutler's office that her breaths warmed his back. He nearly asked why she was behind him, but didn't want her to move away. The elevator jerked to a stop. Nadine bumped into his back, placing her hands on his shoulders.

"Sorry," she said.

"What for? It's this old elevator's fault." Riordan took her hand and led her off the car. He faced her in the hallway outside Cutler's office. She looked down and her eyelashes cast shadows on her cheeks. Despite the game she was playing, he still wanted to be inside her. Wanted to taste her blood. He picked up the ends of her hair, spilling over her right shoulder. "Why do you dye your hair?" He thought about the turquoise beads at this throat that were almost the same color.

"Because there's nothing much I can do about the color of my eyes."

"What's wrong with brown? There are worse colors."

"None more boring."

"I disagree," he said, raising his hand to knock. The door swung open. "Hey."

"Hm...hey," Cutler said, stepping back, allowing Riordan and Nadine inside the office.

"She has something she wants to tell you."

"Yeah," the director said, pursing his lips. He

growled under his breath what was the equivalent of *this-ought-to-be-interesting*.

Again, Nadine stood closely and slightly behind him. Normally, this would have bothered him—someone right up on him like that. Cutler gave him a strange look. Riordan shrugged.

"Speak up, female," Cutler said.

"They have my sister."

"What are you after?" Cutler eyed her suspiciously.

"I'm not after anything."

"Doubtful. What, they only want information?" Nadine didn't respond. "So, not information." She remained mute. "I'm losing my patience, human." His words dripped with menace. "What do they want?" He bared his fangs. Riordan bared his in return.

"They said they'd let us both go if I gave them information."

"About what?" Cutler asked in English then snarled *"She's lying,"* to Riordan.

"I don't know."

Cutler chuckled without humor yet smiled. She inched even closer to Riordan, melding into his backside. He couldn't tell if she was afraid. Bator had a unique language only they understood. Speaking in a series of clicks and snorts, Cutler said, *"Set her up. You know what to do."*

Riordan grunted, "Yes, sir."

Cutler clapped his hands together. "Sorry, we don't negotiate with demons." He turned toward his desk.

"I'm not asking you to."

"We don't negotiate with demons, but we can't let you leave either."

Nadine came out from behind Riordan. "Why not?"

"Because our sworn duty is to protect humans and you're in immediate danger."

"You can't keep me here."

"Yes, we can."

"Under whose authority?"

Cutler's nostrils flared. "Mine!"

"You aren't cops," she snapped. Riordan wanted to tell her to quit it, she was stinking up the place with her bullshit. If she was after something, this wasn't how to get it. Piss Cutler off too much and she'd be back in the straps room.

Riordan placed a hand on her shoulder. "Calm dow—"

"No. I'm not going to calm down. Besides, has saying calm down ever worked?" She shrugged him off.

Okay, that was true right there. Riordan nearly laughed.

"We have jurisdiction when it comes to

protecting humans from demons of a Collective. You will stay here until I tell you, you can leave," Cutler said.

"How do the police feel about you kidnapping people, huh?"

Cutler took a cell phone out of his desk drawer and handed it to her. "Here, call 9-1-1." When she didn't take the phone, he continued. "No? How 'bout I call and tell them we found you driving a stolen vehicle? How does that sound? You want to threaten me some more?"

"You a—"

Riordan growled, cutting her off.

"Get out her out of my office!"

Riordan marched her toward the door. She hung her head down in defeat, however, the gesture didn't seem like something she would do. Not the way she spoke to Cutler just now. She wasn't scared of him. She didn't even seem like the type of woman to back down from a fight. As they passed by, Cutler winked at him.

CHAPTER SIX

RIORDAN

Riordan shut Cutler's door behind them. "Come with me."

"Where are we going? Because if it's back downstairs, forget it. You might as well kill me now and get it over with."

"What? No one's going to kill you." He started walking down the hallway to the stairwell.

After a second, she jogged after him. He stopped at the stairs access.

"Where are we going then?"

"To get something to eat."

"Oh." Nadine put her hands on her neck, looking a tad paler. "You eat...food, right?"

"Yes. Do you eat food?"

She sighed heavily. "You know I do."

"Then why are you asking me, if I eat food?"

"I didn't know if you also ate food."

Riordan laughed. "What else would I eat?"

"I didn't know if you only ate blood."

"We *eat* food. We *drink* blood. You don't know much about Homodae, do you?"

"I've heard that term before. Homodae. It's what you're really called."

Riordan smiled as he placed his palm on the bio scanner, unlocking the door to the stairs. She followed him up to the floor with the cafeteria. The kitchen was open for almost twenty-fours. He took a tray from the stack sitting at the end of the counter. "Grab a tray."

Nadine took one and put it next to his on the tray rack. They shuffled along the open refrigerator, sliding their trays. "What do they have? I mean what's good here?"

"Everything, but I'm partial to hot foods." He whistled for the chef on duty to come out of the back. "Hey, Vince. Can I get that thing I like so much?" He turned to Nadine. "Do you trust me?"

"Uh…"

"Make that two." Riordan held up two fingers.

"Have a seat, I'll bring it out to you."

The cafeteria was empty except for the two of them. He chose a table near the soda machines. Vince brought their food out by the time they sat down after getting something to drink. Nadine stared at the plate in front of her as if she had never seen anything like it before.

"This is what you wanted me to trust you over. A hamburger?"

"Yeah, why? What were you expecting?" He grinned, saliva filling his mouth. He hadn't eaten in a while.

"I dunno. But not this." She smiled for the first time.

"It's the best burger I've ever had. Better than any fast food joint." He took a bite while she stared at him.

"I hate to break it to you but that's not saying a whole heck of a lot."

"Just eat," he said between chews.

* * *

Nadine

Nadine was having by far the strangest night of her life and that included being taken by demons. She wasn't quite sure, but she thought she may have died and the demons brought her back to life. Was she really sitting across from a Homodae? His eyes mesmerized her. She couldn't stop staring.

After finishing their burgers, Riordan showed her a few of his favorite places in the building. The weight training room was as boring as it sounded when he described it to her on the way there. Everything seemed like normal things someone would find in a weight facility. The one exception was the pounds. There wasn't a single thing in there under 100 lbs. including the hand dumbbells. She tried lifting one and failed.

He picked one from the floor like the dumbbell weighed nothing more than an ounce and set it on the rack. How strong were these guys?

"How much can you lift?" she asked.

"Depends on what kind of lifting. Dead lift or bench press?"

"Bench press."

"Seven fifty, sometimes more on a good day."

"Is that a lot?"

He shrugged. "I guess. We have some human employees here, that can do about two fifty to three hundred. I'm told that's decent for them."

She tried thinking about what types of things

equated to seven hundred fifty pounds. *A bear? Pony?* "You're, like, twice as strong as a human?"

"Our females are a bit stronger, but yeah."

"So Kalani can beat you up?"

Riordan snorted. "Only if I didn't fight her back."

"But she is stronger than you?" Nadine made a note to keep away from the female. She slinked toward him, catching their reflections in the mirror covering one entire wall. He stood about a foot or more taller than her. His arms were at his sides and the biceps looked big even while at rest. She circled him, checking out his backside. He whirled around, so he faced her.

"What are you doing?" His irises flared as they had back in front of Sam's house.

"Checking you out."

He gasped quietly.

Taking advantage of Riordan right now to get out of this building probably could work except she still didn't know where the pendant was kept. If she went back to the Collective without any information to offer, they would kill her sister, and likely make her watch or worse, make her do it.

All right, enough playing around. She had a mission to complete. Nadine gathered her hair and pulled it off to one side, exposing her neck. Stepping closer to him, she inhaled his scent. This wasn't something she intended to do and didn't even try to conceal her actions. Ridiculous. His eyes. Oh God, his eyes made everything disappear. She had to keep from looking into them if she wanted to eventually leave. So easily she could stay. Why was she tempted by him? He wasn't human. Well, he was part human, but mostly demon, and a descendant of an Egyptian deity.

As a child, she remembered learning about the Homodae in school. What they were, how they were created. They didn't then and still didn't have the right to vote, and were considered property of the U.S. government. Even the ones that chose to emancipate themselves from the "program." They were labeled feral. Many years later, people continue fearing them, believing they were wild animals and kept caged in this building until they were called upon by duty.

"What made you decide to stay with the program?" she asked. "I remember reading in school that you could choose to leave when you turn sixteen."

He shrugged. "Where would I go?"

"Anywhere."

He cocked his head. "What makes you bring this up now?"

"I always wondered what keeps Bator in line."

"In line? Why, do you know of some that aren't?"

"No. You know how humans view you, right? As

wild animals that need to be locked in cages during the day."

Riordan laughed. "I don't care."

"How can you not care?"

"Why do you?" The door to gym opened and Kalani entered. Nadine stared at her. The Bator females had somewhat petite frames, but there was nothing little about this one. She had gobs of flowing black hair. And her eyes shined red-orange. Kalani's workout clothes showed off her spindly but solid muscled arms and her six-pack abs. Nadine covered her stomach. Even though she was thin, a twinge of self-consciousness fluttered in her mind. The phrase 'skinny fat' got tossed around too.

"Does your stomach hurt?" Riordan asked.

Why would my stom—oh. She removed her hands from across her middle. "Uh uh." When she turned her head, she expected him to be standing next to her. He'd moved to spot Kalani on the bench press, who laid on the padded bench, waiting for him to help her hoist the bar off the cups.

"Thanks," Kalani said as he released the barbell to her completely. With little exertion, she raised and lowered the heavy weight.

Nadine could barely lift fifty pounds without injuring herself. Humans were weak. No wonder they needed a specialized force to protect them. Riordan stood over the bench, his eyes holding steady on the barbell. She followed his line of vision and discovered he wasn't in fact watching the weight, but the female. His lips parted. Had his fangs descended too? She needed to know. Nadine moved closer. Only the tips showed. Which meant they hadn't lowered fully. He was having a reaction to her of some sort though. As she opened her mouth another Bator male marched into the room.

This guy was taller than Riordan. "Take a break. I got this," he said. He glanced at her. Jerking his chin, he said, "What's she doing here?"

"You know what she's doing here. Cutler wanted her brought in."

"I know that. What's she doing in this room?"

"I'm showing her around." After Riordan finished what he'd said in English, he followed it with a round of random clicking and popping noises from deep within his throat. They had a language only other Homodae understood. Humans had never been able to decode the sounds. Basically, they could be plotting to take over the world and humans would never know. However, realistically, if that was the case, they would have done so already.

The taller male Nadine didn't know grunted then refocused his attention on Kalani. He aided her in returning the barbell to the holders. Leaning over the bar, he kissed her as she rose to meet his mouth.

Annnd...Riordan stared at the obvious couple

the entire time. Why this made Nadine jealous annoyed her. She snapped her fingers in front of his face. Breaking from his trance, he motioned for her to follow him. "Let's go."

"Yeah. Let's." Nadine smirked behind his back until out in the hallway.

CHAPTER SEVEN

RIORDAN

Riordan white-knuckle gripped the beads of his black hemp necklace. Kalani was Dru's mate. Period. That wasn't going to change, and she seemed oblivious that Riordan wanted to punch his best friend every time he saw them together.

At the bank of elevators, he pressed his hand to the bio-scanner.

"What are you showing me next?" Nadine asked.

"Nothing. I'm tired." When the elevator arrived, he pulled her inside.

"Nothing? This is a huge building, there must be other things..."

The glare he gave her shut her up. He hit the button for his floor.

"Where are you taking me then?" she asked.

"Up."

"That would lead to *where*, exactly?"

"My apartment."

"Oh. You want to show me your apartment?" She twirled the ends of her hair around her index finger.

"I'm exhausted and I'm not leaving you to wander around alone."

"Why don't you trust—"

Riordan growled, slammed his palm on the 'STOP' button, and backed her into the corner, trapping her there. The elevator lurched to a halt. "You don't especially evoke trust in me."

"But we shared a moment downstairs?"

"If you're talking about in the straps room, don't mistake lust for feelings." He smelled his own bullshit. His protective instinct had come alive the moment they met. Why was he drawn to her? When he had been watching Kalani during her bench press reps, his attraction for her was there, but it didn't have the intensity it once had. She was gorgeous, yes, but Nadine made him soar. Staring at her, he ran his tongue over his fangs. They tingled and eased down, forcing his mouth open.

Nadine flashed her throat and he wasn't sure if she was aware of it either. Her jugular pulsed under the skin, calling to him like the last drop of drinkable water on the planet. His body went hard. Every part.

She swallowed, bringing her eyes up to meet his. "How long are you going to keep me trapped here?"

"Forever."

"That's a long time. I meant in this elevator."

He licked his lips. "I wanna taste you." He picked her up with his hands under her ass and pressed her against the wall with his hips. She gasped, putting her hands on his shoulders, not pushing him away, yet not inviting him to feed.

"How often do you need it?"

"I don't know." He assumed a lot. How would he know? Riordan's chest vibrated as he purred.

"You don't know? How is that poss—"

"We can find out."

"What if it's too much for me?"

In some ways, Riordan couldn't believe the conversation they were having. A new surge of blood traveled south, making his leather pants tighter. "I don't think anyone has died from too much."

She paled. "Yeah...y-yeah, they have, I've seen—"

"Who do you know that has died from too much?" He thought for a second. "Okay, maybe from a heart attack during or right after."

"People have had heart attacks?"

"No one I know." He pushed his hips forward. Even though he'd never done it, the more instinctual part of him wasn't nervous. Thank the gods. "I promise I won't hurt you."

"But it stings, right?"

"I've never heard that before."

"But you said it does, downstairs."

"What are you talking about? When have we ever had this conversation?" *Oh.* "You mean in the straps room?" He eased her to the floor then leaned over and hit the 'RUN' button. The hair flopped over his forehead flew up when he sighed heavily. He adjusted the front of his pants. Zero to sixty... sixty to zero.

* * *

Nadine

The silence dragged as they elevator went up. Whether his bite stung was a legit question. She wanted to let him feed, the idea turned her on. Much more than she wanted to admit. So much more. The elevator arrived at his floor.

"What happened there?" she asked as they stepped into a hallway. Their shoes squeaked on the tile. She glanced around. What was this place? It looked like an institution, like a hospital ward. Light beige paint covered the walls. Florescent fixtures ran down the center of a drop ceiling. "I thought you said we were going to your apartment?"

Two doors away from the elevators they stopped. "Home sweet home," he said, opening the door. People believed Bator lived in cages. What she thought was a rumor wasn't far from the truth. Stark. Unadorned. Windowless. Nothing about the apartment, if you could call it that, said home or sweet.

"You live here?" She slapped her hand over her mouth, having not meant to say that out loud. "Sorry."

He snorted-chuckled. "It's all right. Not what you expected, huh?"

Beneath her feet lay the same tile as in the hallway. Riordan brushed past her and sat on the king-sized bed pushed against the wall. He eased onto his back with his legs still over the end of the bed. Gripping the choker around his neck by the beads, he yanked, ripping the black cord off. He tossed the necklace across the room.

They stared at each other. Minutes ticked by before she spoke. His eyes smoldered.

"How come you took your necklace off?

"Don't need it."

"It's just that I see you play with the beads a lot."

"It was only some stupid craft project."

Nadine giggled. "Craft project?"

"Yeah, well, never mind."

She nodded. He didn't want to talk about it. Got it. "You never answered, what happened in the elevator?"

He paused before responding. "A miscommunication."

"How so? You said you wanted to taste me. How was that a miscommunication? I thought that was pretty clear."

"I do."

"Am I missing something?"

"I don't know, are you?"

"Why are you being like this...?" *Ah, crap.* They had had a lot of talk about 'it'. "When I said 'it' you thought I meant sex."

"Like I said, Teal, miscommunication." He stood. And. He. Was. Tall. Damn near a foot taller than her.

Nadine had been about to tell him not to call her Teal when took his shirt off. "Holy crap, you're like a...a work of art." She wished she could, growl, purr like him, or at the least whistle. Anything. Shout from the rooftops, "Homodae are beautiful!" Her cheeks heated. What did the rest of him look like? "Take your pants off."

Wait. Dammit.

She was making a habit of blurting things out.

"You want me to take my pants off?"

"Yes."

Uh! She did it again. The male messed with her head. *Stay focused.* She needed to be sharp. Her sister was counting on her. Oh, but maybe just this once. After all, she needed to snoop around the building without a chaperone. Give in to him, because come on, she wanted him so badly. Wait for him to fall asleep then slip out of the room, hopefully find the pendant, then escape. How hard could that be?

She crossed her arms. "I'm waiting."

He shrugged and tugged at his waistband. Teasing her, not really unbuttoning them. Jesus. "Are you sure you want this?" he asked.

She nodded because she didn't trust anything that would come out of her mouth, like "I love you," and "I never want to leave this place again." Absurd, really. Or was it? He scared her in many ways but none of them physical. She wanted to be near him. Craved his scent. She almost laughed out loud. Who was she, Edward from *Twilight*? They weren't even vampires. Okay, Homodae had vampire qualities due to their ancestry. Riordan wouldn't live forever? Oh, who cared? This was one night because that's all she had. She'd die to get her sister out of the Collective.

He opened the fly of his pants and stood there expectantly as if waiting for her next command.

"Take them off."

"All right, you asked for it."

What did he mean?

He slid his leather pants down his legs.

My God.

When he stepped out of the pants pooled at his feet and stood to his full height, he was gloriously naked.

Good...God.

Nadine had been with some men that worked out and even a personal trainer where all he did was lift weights and train. But Homodae, or at least this one, was incredible. Riordan had not skipped leg day either. He had tree trunks for thighs. Oh man, she thought she had appreciated his body clothed. His abs rippled as he breathed heavily.

"Can I touch you?" she asked.

"You can do whatever you want."

Whatever, I want.

"Tie you up and spank you?"

He smiled, and his body flushed. His erection

bobbed as he rocked side to side. "Maybe not the first time."

Crossing the room, she went to him. She ran her hands down his chest, over his stomach, her fingers catching on every groove in his six pack, until she reached his...oh lordy, yes... He gasped as she palmed him. Her clothes scratched her skin, every inch of her tingled with desire. Riordan's eyes closed, shutting off the amber glow.

"Open your eyes," she whispered. "I want to see them." His cat-like pupils had dilated. For some reason, she wondered why Homodae had slits in their eyes, although Egyptians did have a history of worshiping cats, and she'd noticed several wandering the building during Riordan's tour.

Reaching up on her tiptoes she kissed his chest right over his heart, walking him backward to the bed. "Lie down." He obeyed without a word. His eyes stayed on her as she stripped. She crawled over him, keeping one knee on each side of him. His hips flexed as she kissed his thighs. If that excited him then...

She swirled her tongue around the tip of his cock. He groaned thrusting toward her. Her own toes curled. "You like that?"

The sound he gave in return reminded her of a lion devouring its prey, yet he could have said something in his language too. Loving the noises he made, she continued pleasuring him.

A cat meowed next to them. Riordan shooed the shiny black furred animal away with his hand. It hissed and jumped off the bed. Funny how she hadn't smelled the feline earlier. She usually had a nose for kitty litter. She had hated dirty things for as long as she could remember. Over the years, she had grown more tolerant, but avoided dirt whenever possible. She moved so her face hovered over his. "I didn't know you had a cat. Where do you keep the litter?"

"What? Why are you asking?" he said breathlessly.

"I didn't smell it."

He chuckled softly. "That's because there is none. Do you really want to talk about this now?" His hands rubbed her back, traveling toward her nape.

"I guess not. It's just that it's gross."

He laughed. "And it bothers you that it might be in this room."

"Yes."

CHAPTER EIGHT

RIORDAN

Riordan got the answer of how Nadine survived the Collective without becoming catatonic. A part of her was demon, Kalani had been right. In the background search, he'd come across her adoption records. He had pushed it aside, not believing it had any significance. However, she had been abandoned by her biological parents and found on the side of the highway as a baby. She was part human based on her lack of purple glowing eyes.

He thought about whether this mattered to him—her being part demon. He smoothed his hands down her hips. Nope. Chances were she didn't even know what she was.

"Kiss me," he said, raising his head.

She brought her mouth down on his. He parted his lips, conscious of his fangs as her tongue slipped inside.

"Bite me," she said between kisses.

The second his fangs grazed her skin, she tensed.

"It won't hurt if you relax."

"You said it stings."

"All cuts sting, try to relax."

Her shoulder and back muscles eased under his hands. "That's it. Now stay with me."

Nadine's hands clutched his forearms. "Just do it, don't tell me when."

Massaging the sides of her neck, he pulled her closer. He struck her vein and sucked. Blood flowed down the back of his throat. His hips raised off the mattress. She whimpered, and her muscles stiffened, but with a mouthful he couldn't assure her he wouldn't take too much. He caressed the back of her neck.

Again, her tension eased. She moved her slick core back and forth over the underside of him. He nearly broke the seal on her neck. Any more of that and he'd lose it. As he reached between them, she understood what he wanted.

"Let me help you with that," she said. And she did. She joined them. They moved together, instinct and need driving him. Could she tell he was a virgin? He had no clue what he was doing, he only knew what felt good.

He removed his fangs from her neck and licked the punctures closed. She sat up, placing her hands on his chest. The new angle brought with it a different sort of friction. Gripping her thighs, he thrusted his hips up. Her breaths increased. Everything becoming more intense. Hotter. Wetter. Pitching her head back, she cried out. That was when it happened. What he'd always heard about from other Bator but hadn't experienced himself. A pillow of air lifted him from the mattress, except he knew he was still lying on the bed. He pulled her on to his chest and wrapped his arms around her, afraid she'd float away. With a growl, he rolled them over. Holding himself up by his hands on either side of her head, he smiled at her.

"Your eyes, they're beautiful," she said, putting her palm up to his cheek.

He leaned into her touch. "So are yours."

"No they aren't. Boring brown."

"How can you say that? And I wouldn't call them boring brown."

"Then what would you call them?"

"Russet." He slowly started moving inside her.

She moaned. "I never thought of them as any color other than brown."

He bit his bottom lip, groaning. "More than one shade of—oh gods." She grabbed his ass and he sucked in a breath. Something about the way she touched him made his skin tingle. He pumped harder, his orgasm gathering in a swell of pleasure. She writhed beneath him, meeting his thrusts. His vision fuzzed, and he collapsed to his elbows. Wondering if Nadine was all right, he glanced at her face. "Nadine, are you...okay?"

She nodded and arched her back. Thank gods, because he wasn't sure he'd be able to stop without hurting himself to do it. Warmth swept through his body. She held on tightly to his biceps. As he drove her into the mattress, she shouted his name once more. Her body began pulsating around him. The floating sensation returned. Did she feel it too?

"Don't let go," she said.

"Never. I've got you," he whispered in her ear. The need for release overtook his movements. Throwing his back, he roared. He came. Hard.

Riordan rolled off Nadine and laid on his side. Beads of sweat slid across his chest, absorbing into the sheets. After a few minutes, his breathing slowed to a normal pace.

"You okay? I didn't hurt you, did I?" he asked.

"Uh uh." She smiled widely. "How did I taste?"

"You have to ask? Fantastic." She did too. Meteoric. "Come here." He opened his arms for her and she came to him like water. She rested her head on his chest while he stroked her back.

CHAPTER NINE

NADINE

Nadine's eyelids drooped. *No.* She couldn't fall asleep, he sister needed her to find that pendant. Lying next to her in bed, Riordan breathed evenly. He'd been doing so for a while now. She wanted to make sure he was completely out before slipping from the room.

Black Cat, as she called her new feline friend,

lay curled on Nadine's left side, flipping its tail up and down and purring. Rolling onto her side, she faced Cat. "So, we finally meet face-to-face," she whispered. She reached her hand out to pet the shiny black fur and it yowled at her. "Okay, I won't touch you."

Cat leaned to the side, licking his paw. She decided he must be a guy cat for no reason other than he seemed to have a male demeanor. He resumed purring and lazily wagging his tail. Although, he looked relaxed, she imagined it was only an act. Cat stood, or in this case, laid sentry, ready to pounce if necessary. He hairy eyeballed her.

Nadine checked on Riordan. She admired his handsome face. As much she wanted to stay with Riordan, love Riordan, she loved her sister more. Or was it different? But what was she thinking about? How could she love him. They had only met...how long had she been here? She didn't remember seeing a clock anywhere and the place didn't have much in the way of windows.

She brushed a whisper of a kiss on his shoulder. *I'm sorry, but I can't stay.*

Ever so gently, she inched toward the foot of the bed. Cat cocked his head. After dressing, she tiptoed to the door. Three feet before her escape, Cat put himself in front of the door and sat. He stared at her with his big green eyes.

"Penny needs me," she said softly. "You'll explain it to him, won't you?"

Stepping around Cat, she opened the door and peered into the hallway. Empty.

One glance back at Riordan, and she slipped out of the tiny apartment. Her chest constricted, tightening and squeezing her lungs until she coughed just to breathe. She walked on the balls of her feet away from Riordan's door. Leaning one hand on the wall, she panted. Her heart raced. What was with her? One night with the guy and she was having a panic attack because she might never see him again?

At the bank of elevators, she examined the bio-scanner.

Shit.

What would happen if she placed her hand on the glass plate? Would an alarm sound because she wasn't an authorized user? What the hell, she could tell Riordan she was thirsty. Nadine put her palm on the scanner. A green light glowed from behind the glass but soon faded. Well, that was anticlimactic. Across the hallway and about ten feet away was the stair access door, and it too had a bio-scanner.

Glancing in the direction of Riordan's door, Cat stuck his head out a kitty door. For the first time she noticed that most of the doors in the corridor had small square flaps near the bottom. He meowed and trotted toward her.

"Hi there," she said as he rubbed against her legs. "Do you know a secret way out of here?"

Meow.

"Where? Show me?" She was talking to a cat and assuming he understood English and knew how to get off this floor.

Cat meowed again and padded down the hall. He stopped and looked at her.

"You want me to follow you?"

Meow.

No way Cat wanted to help, he was probably leading her to Cutler. He had a menacing vibe to him. His voice was so damn deep, he sounded like Darth Vader. And his growl. She shivered. Nonetheless, she followed the cat.

He took her to another nondescript door. Big surprise. The place was so devoid of warmth she wondered why anyone would choose to stay there. Cat pushed through the kitty door while she tried the doorknob which was...unlocked. Inside the closet, she found a laundry shoot and soda and ice machines.

Cat stood on his hind legs with his paws on the wall below the laundry chute. Yep, she knew it. The cat wanted her dead.

"You can't be serious? You want me to slide

down this hole?" Nadine stuck her head in the chute, peering down. The shaft appeared wide enough for her to fit but where did the chute lead?

Screw it.

Out of options, she put one leg into the chute, held onto the wood trim framing the hole, and pulled her other leg inside. She lowered herself into the metal lined shaft, turning at the same time so she could hook her fingers on the lip of the chute. "For Penny," she said, letting go.

She dropped ten feet or so before the panic set in. What if nothing was at the bottom to break her fall? No doubt Cat was up there laughing and thinking: *Ha! That's what you get, stupid human, for following a domestic animal.* How incredibly easy she'd fallen into a trap. Nadine put her hands and feet out to the sides, hoping they would act as breaks and either slow her down or stop the slide before she plummeted to her death. However, the sides of the slide of death proved too slick and she continued falling.

She landed in an overloaded bin of clothing, smacking her wrist on the metal rim. "Oww!" Tears filled her eyes. Nadine cradled her left arm. Her wrist swelled immediately. She knew it was broken the second she wiggled her fingers. Pain shot all the way up to her shoulder. Great. Survive the fall and break a bone. She looked around for something to splint her wrist with. However, the only things in the room were washer and dryers, a stainless steel table for folding clothes, and more large bins like the one she was in.

Bracing for the pain, Nadine climbed out, using one hand for support. She nearly faceplanted on the cement floor as she became lightheaded for a moment. Her chin quivered. "Fuck, it hurts."

She pictured Cat laughing again. With tears in her eyes, she lumbered to the only door, babying her wrist.

All right, man up.

Holding her breath, she twisted the doorknob and what do you know, it opened. A bio-scanner hung from the wall outside the laundry room. Someone could leave the room but couldn't get in?

She worked her way down the hallway, looking through the tiny glass window in each door she passed. At the end of the corridor was a stairwell without a door or stupid bio scanner keeping her out. She climbed several flights and stopped at the first floor that didn't have a scanner next to the door.

Holding her breath, she pushed open the door. The hallway was dark, except for the red glow of an emergency exit sign above a door at the far side, and blue light emanating from a room with a large window across from her.

And what do we have here?

The light glowed brightly then dimmed. She crept closer to the glass and peered inside the room. In a glass box sat a shiny necklace. This had to be the pendant. The door was secured with a bio scanner. Dammit.

Defeated, she leaned against the wall, trying to come up with an excuse to tell Riordan about how she broke her arm and praying he would buy it. She turned her head side to side as a stiffness settled in her neck, most likely from her fall. There, attached to the cinderblock wall, hung a fire extinguisher.

With renewed purpose, she grabbed the fire extinguisher from the hook. Fortunately, it didn't weigh as much as she thought it would. She swung the red container by the hose and smacked the glass. A spider web crack formed in the window. On the second swing, the glass crumbled. Using the butt of the extinguisher, she cleared the glass fragments from around the frame. Reaching through the glassless window, Nadine unlocked the door from the inside.

To her surprise, no alarms sounded. Although there could have been a silent one. She had no time to worry about that though. She lifted the lid on the pendant's glass box and the glow died. She grabbed the necklace and shoved it into the front pocket of her jeans.

Now, how the hell did she get out of there?

Meow.

Cat weaved back and forth through her legs. "You wanna help me again? Oh, good, you do."

The cat trotted away, and she followed.

* * *

The cat led her down the stairs she'd come from, but didn't stop on the same floor as the laundry. They went one floor past that. He showed her a vent covered with a thin slatted grate. Cold air blew out of it. She inspected the cover and found only one screw held it in place. Wedging one hand under the cover, she pulled up. The screw easily detached from the wall.

The vent was a little wider than the laundry chute. She shimmied her way through the vent until she reached another slatted grate. A strange metallic smell tickled her nose. She held her breath and punched the vent cover with both feet, knocking it off.

Splash. Bang.

Nadine set her feet down in a three-inch puddle of water covering the ground all around her. Ew. The water seeped through the canvas of her shoes. Wherever she was smelled of old pennies, and the walls were made of dark bricks with fat lines of mortar between them. A thick beam of light shone through a square hole above her. As she neared the opening, she realized it was a storm drain cover.

She wobbled as a dizziness came over her. A few unsteady steps forward and she fell on her ass in the stinky, dirty water. She shuddered. However, her nightmare was only beginning. Her body went limp, her arms feeling heavier, and she had trouble sitting up. The concern over what was happening paled next to idea of losing consciousness in a place full of filthy water.

Unable to stay awake, she collapsed the rest of the way to the water covered cement.

CHAPTER TEN

RIORDAN

There was knock on Riordan's door. He sat upright in bed. The first thing he did was search for Nadine. Like he could have predicted but hoped he was wrong about, the bed was empty except for him.

Knock. Knock.

"Riory?" Kalani said from out in the hallway.

"Gimme a minute. I need to put some pants on."

"Really," she said impatiently. "Why do you need to put pants on, huh?"

Riordan hissed loudly enough for her to hear and yanked the door open. She held a passed out Nadine.

"I found her in the drainage tunnel, out cold. I think she broke her wrist, it doesn't look too good."

"Gods! How did she get down there?"

"How should I know? But she set off the alarm."

Riordan had a suspicion who led her there. Crazy as it sounded, his cat was most likely responsible. She sensed things. Knew things no one else did. Bastet trotted into the room through Kalani's feet with a smugness about her. Man, he should have known his cat had something to do with it. She was clever, and he often thought Bastet was smarter than him. "What did you do, try to get rid of her? Didn't think about the sleep gas in the drain, did you?"

"Uh, you know she's just a cat, right? She can't actually answer you. Or speak English." Kalani laid Nadine on the bed.

"Keep telling yourself that," Riordan said. He knew the cats in this building weren't ordinary even if no one except Dru and Cutler believed him. Bastet jumped on the bed and laid next to Nadine and put a paw on her stomach. He scowled at the cat. "Don't touch her." She hissed back. "I don't know why you're hissing."

I already know she's a demon.

"Hey, I found this on her." Kalani dangled the pendant she'd stolen from the demon Collective leader in front of him.

"I figured. So?"

"She was trying to steal it."

"I realize that." Riordan examined her badly swollen wrist. Definitely broken. He feared hurting her by moving the arm.

"How did she even know where to find it?" Kalani asked.

Eyeing the cat, he said, "I wonder."

"Don't tell me you think Bastet showed her?"

The cat lifted her paw from Nadine's middle, returning it with her claws out. She didn't dig the nails in, merely tested how far she could push Riordan. He glared at Bastet, baring his fangs. The claws retracted. "Why don't you like her?" As he kneeled next to Nadine on the floor, Bastet went to him, purring, rubbing her sides on him as if marking him. "Oh, I see, you're jealous."

Crossing her arms over her chest, Kalani sighed loudly. Riordan had been studiously ignoring her presence.

"Did anyone else see you with her?"

"Cutler. He told me she was your responsibility and to bring her to you. But I don't get it."

"There are things you don't understand."

"Don't patronize me. What's going on?"

"He isn't sure yet and doesn't trust anyone."

"Trust anyone, who?"

"The humans who created us," he whispered.

Kalani's face tightened in confusion. "I'm sorry, what are you saying?"

"I'm saying," he lowered his voice, "that the pendant you took—something's up with it."

"Well, yeah, it has the same symbol on it as the Guard's logo. I've been doing some research in the library—"

"The library here?"

"Gods, no. Public library."

"You know, it wasn't an accident, I survived the Collective's realm without losing my mind."

At the same time, they both said, "We *are* part demon." Riordan sensed Nadine waking. The blood he had drank from her connected them. He wondered if she felt the link too. She laid still though.

"So what did you find out?" he asked Kalani.

"I think demons stole the necklace from us, or our people. Like it's some sort of relic, believed to hold a power. I saw something similar in one of the books I read."

"What kind of power?"

She shrugged. "I dunno, but clearly the demons want it back."

"I'm sure it's not the only thing."

Kalani rolled her eyes. "I know I'm a target, so what? Aren't we all?"

She had a point. Demons wanted them dead because they kept their population down and made the access to blood more difficult. Riordan nodded. "Lemme see that thing." He held out his hand for the pendant Nadine tried getting away with. "This is a fake you know, a decoy." Yes, he knew Nadine was listening. "Cutler wanted to see if she'd take the bait."

"Now that she has?" Kalani asked.

"Nothing. If the Collective wants it back, we'll give it to them."

"So we are going to let her take them a fake? You know they will kill her once they get it back."

"Not if we trade with the real one."

"So, you're telling me you want to give them the real deal?"

"I don't want to, but what choice do we have?"

"Where is it?"

* * *

Nadine

Nadine had seen the pendant glow, hadn't she? The glass box certainly had. How could it be fake? She laid still, trying not make a sound or move a muscle.

But a sensation she couldn't quite describe, buzzed inside her. It was like...

"I keep it right here," Riordan said.

Nadine popped one eyelid open. He walked across to the dresser with Kalani following him. A pendant swung from a chain between his fingers as he turned toward the female Bator. Light from overhead glinted off the shiny metal surface. It looked like the same one she had taken earlier.

"After we dug into Nadine's past, we decided to bring her here, see what she—"

"What she does," Kalani finished his sentence.

"Yes. Exactly."

Nadine gasped at the coldness in his voice. And to think she *wanted* to have sex with him. Enjoyed it even. Really enjoyed it. Oh. God. Yes. She sat up on the bed. *Whoa.* Blood rushed to her head. Shooting pains radiated upward from her wrist. A dizziness sent her crashing back onto the mattress.

"Welcome back," he said, smiling. The tips of his fangs showed. Demons didn't have sharp pointed canines or whatever. She pressed her tongue to her eyeteeth. Yep, although slightly pointed, still dull. For no reason whatsoever, Nadine wanted his fangs sunk into her neck again. What was wrong with her? He was using her. She had used him, though.

He lunged for her. Okay, maybe he did care.

Squatting next to the bed, he stroked her hair.

"My wrist hurts," Nadine said.

"Let me take you downstairs and get you—"

Her chin quivered. "I don't want to go to the straps room...please."

"I was going to say, get you looked at. We have medical staff that work here."

"Human or Homodae?"

"When have you ever known one of us to go to medical school?"

"So human?"

"Yes." He grinned. "Human."

"Why do you want to get my wrist looked at?"

"Do you mean why do I care when you tried stealing the pendant?"

"Yeah," she said softly.

"Yeah, why?" Kalani interjected.

Riordan whirled on Kalani. "If you don't like the way I do things, then leave my apartment. She's injured, and I don't give a shit how it happened. Our sworn duty is to protect and aid humans. Did you forget?"

Kalani gave him a look of surprise then spun, heading for the door.

Nadine frowned. Oh, so that was why he was being nice, it was his duty.

Don't do me any favors, buddy.

She found a tiny sliver of strength, pulled herself upright again, and swung her feet over the side of the bed. What in the hell was in that storm drain? Her energy faded before she could stand. "What's wrong...with me?" She fell against the mattress.

"Sleep gas."

"I feel like I've been anesth...anesthetized."

"Something like that. Come on," he said, scooping her in his arms.

Nadine groaned when her wrist jostled.

CHAPTER ELEVEN

RIORDAN

"Are you sure this is okay?" Nadine asked Riordan.

"You want your wrist fixed, don't you?" They passed Jade's room. Cutler sat in a chair next to the bed, feeding her something out of a bowl.

One of the medical staff stood at the end the of the hallway speaking with his favorite doctor.

"Hey, doc," Riordan called, "can you help us out?"

The guy raised a finger indicating he needed a minute. Riordan ducked into the exam room across the hall from Jade's.

Doctor Bowman came in right after Riordan had laid Nadine on the padded table. "What seems to be the problem, Riory?" The doctor looked him over like he was the patient and not the one lying down.

"Not me, her."

"Yes, I was only kidding." He stepped around Riordan. "What can I help you with, uh...?"

"Nadine," said Riordan. "It's her wrist."

Gently, the doctor squeezed her wrist with his fingers. "Does this hurt?"

"Yow!" Nadine gasped, tears springing to her eyes.

"A lot, apparently. It may be broken, but I'll need to take an x-ray to know for sure. Can you sit up for me?"

"Not especially, they gassed me."

The doctor glanced sideways at Riordan.

"Drainage tunnel."

Nodding, the doctor helped her sit up. "The effects will wear off by tomorrow."

"Tomorrow?"

Doctor Bowman nodded. "Considering that you

either were breaking in or out, I don't think you'll be leaving anytime soon."

"No offense," Nadine said, "but I don't think that's up to you."

"Can you just examine her wrist and mind your own business?" Riordan said impatiently.

* * *

An hour later, Riordan and Nadine headed for the elevators. She had opted to walk instead of being carried. Halfway there, her legs gave out and she scrambled for his arm, something to hang onto.

"Told you I should carry you."

"Shut up, this is your fault."

"What is my fault? I didn't make you break your wrist. How did you do it anyway?"

"The gas, not my wrist. I know that was my fault."

"First of all, the gas is always present there and second—well there isn't a second, but I'm sure I'll think of one later."

The elevator doors slid open and he pulled her onto the elevator with him.

"Listen, do you still want to get your sister out of the Collective?"

"Yes."

"By the way, you can probably speed up the healing process by taking some of my blood."

Nadine remained silent, and by her expression he couldn't tell what she was thinking. Was she grossed out? Was she scared because she craved his blood? What?

They arrived at his floor and he practically carried her to the apartment. Once inside, she shuffled to the bed, collapsing on top.

"You never gave me an answer."

"I wasn't aware you had asked a question."

"Do you want some of my blood? It'll help you."

And help me keep even better track of you too.

"Not sure I can stomach anymore of that stuff."

"You've had Red before?"

Her eyebrows knitted together. "By 'Red' I'm assuming you mean blood from a Homodae?"

Gods, he loved when she used their true species name. It made him respect her more. "Yes, but directly from my vein, none of the bagged stuff."

"I don't have fangs."

He smiled. "I know."

"Will I grow them?"

He smirked. "No. Why would you think that?"

"If you think it will help, but I'm not sure I won't throw up." She made a gagging gesture by sticking her tongue out and putting her hand to the base of her throat.

"Why do think you'll puke?"

"The demons forced me to drink theirs. Blood's blood, right?"

"I don't think in this case that's true." The fact that she had blunt teeth instead of sharp fangs made him want her to bite him. Hard. On the ass. "And my blood isn't purple."

"What color is it?"

"Um, red," he said incredulously.

Wiggling her fingers, she winced.

"Look, clearly your arm hurts. Do you want some of my blood or not?"

"How will this work? Give me a glass or—"

Bringing his wrist to his mouth, Riordan bit into his flesh. Blood welled from the two puncture wounds and dripped onto the floor. "Here, drink."

"How do I—"

"You suck." When she remained prone on the bed, he went over and propped her torso off the mattress. Although, she hadn't averted her head, she didn't drink either. "The wound is going to close soon if you don't start sucking."

Drops of blood fell, absorbing into her shirt. She licked her lips and drew in a short breath. Her tongue snaked out and she lapped the punctures. "That's—it tastes—wow, not what I expected."

"Is that good or bad?"

"Good," she said, forming a seal over the bite

marks. She sucked, pulling long drags of blood into her mouth.

Riordan tilted his head back and gasped. He broke out into a sweat. Heat flooded his entire body, which screamed to get inside hers. With every mouthful she swallowed, their connection deepened until he nearly heard the whispers of her thoughts.

Nadine began moaning, gripping his arm tighter. After one final pull of blood, she released the seal on his wrist with a hiss. A line of blood ran down her chin from the corner of her mouth. It was the hottest thing he had ever seen.

"You have a..." he brushed his own face where the line of blood streaked her face.

She ran an index finger over the blood from chin to the corner of her mouth, and licked the blood from her finger. The whole time Nadine kept her eyes on him. "Thanks." He took it back, *that* was the hottest thing he'd ever seen.

Riordan stood and straightened the front of his pants. Putting *things* in a more comfortable position.

"What's the matter, did your pants get tighter?"

He cleared his throat. "Yes."

She giggled. "Did that really turn you on, me drinking your blood?"

"Yes. How did it feel when I drank from you?"

"Erotic as hell."

"How do you feel now?"

"My wrist doesn't throb like it has its own heartbeat anymore."

* * *

Nadine

Oh, God.

The way he looked at her with half-mast eyes, she almost forgot about how she was being used. They wanted her returning the pendant to the Collective. Nadine wasn't sure why the demons wanted it in the first place. The symbol was the same as the Bator Patrol Guard. But if it had some type of special power, then wanting the stupid thing made sense.

Riordan riffled through his top dresser drawer. With his back to her, she couldn't tell what he was doing. He slid the drawer closed and opened the next one down, pulling out a pair of sweatpants. "I'm going to take a shower, if you want one I might have a t-shirt you can wear. Or Kalani may have something too."

"Why are you lying to me?"

Shutting the drawer, he turned toward her. "What do you think I lied to you about?"

"The pendant I stole wasn't fake."

"You heard us talking?"

"Yeah. When were you going to tell me? And spare me that you were lying to Kalani because of some not trusting anyone bullshit."

Riordan sighed, adding a groan to the end.

"Yeah, that's right, groan all you want. I see how you look at her."

"How do I look at her?"

"Like you want her to be your next meal."

"I *don't* look at her like that." He shoved his fists down to his sides. His irises flared, the slit-pupils widening. "I want *you* to be my next meal."

Man, she wanted to be too, getting a vision of her legs cranked open and his head between her thighs. But no, she wanted to throw some shit across the room. She stood and got up in his face. The scent of him piqued her arousal. Why did she want him so badly? Her body craved his. Was it the blood? No, this had also happened before she drank from him.

Riordan pulled open the second drawer. He tossed one of the necklaces to her. "This is the real one, the one you tried stealing. The chain is heavier than the decoy." After opening the top drawer, he paused. "I want you to give the demons the real one tomorrow," he said, throwing the fake at her.

She tested the weight of each in her hands. "Why would you do this, and I know it's not because you want to."

"I'm not interested in gambling with anyone's life."

"Won't you get in trouble?"

"That's my decision, not yours. I took an oath to serve and protect humans."

"But you were going to—"

"I changed my mind."

Chapter Twelve

RIORDAN

Gods, Penny's life was over even if they used the real pendant in exchange for her freedom. Life after a Collective for a human wasn't living, only existing. Jade had lain in the bed downstairs day in and day out, never changing, never showing any signs of improvement. They had to try with Nadine's sister though, even if the outlook was grim.

Nadine leapt off the bed, rushing him. She threw her arms around his chest.

"Yeah, it's—you're welcome."

His body caught fire as she hugged him tighter. He gasped. This probably wasn't the effect she was going for, nonetheless his entire body tensed with desire to the point that he might die if he didn't have her at least one more time. After tomorrow, they both might be dead. Picking her head off his bare chest, she looked at him, smoothing her hands around his back and down over his ass. "Do you still want me to be your next meal?"

Closing his eyes, Riordan moaned.

More than you know.

"You said something about a shower," she said, leading him into the bathroom. "Will you wash my back?"

"Anything you want, I'm yours." *Er...shit, why did I say that?* "I mean, I want to be yours—I mean... fuck. That's not what I—"

Nadine giggled and turned on the shower. "Oh crap, I forgot about this cast."

"Fiberglass, it'll be all right."

After taking off her clothes, Nadine stepped over the lip of the tub. The water ran over her delicious curves. Pivoting, she used the hand without the cast to rinse her hair. "Are you joining me or are you going to stand there staring at me with your mouth open?"

Riordan ditched his sweats and slid in beside her. She pressed her wet body against his, putting her arms around his neck. He nuzzled into the crook of her neck, kissing and nipping her with his fangs.

Her body undulated in his arms, rubbing him in the right places. They kissed until her lips became puffy and rosy. He broke from her and grabbed the shampoo bottle, squeezing some into his hand. After soaping her teal hair, he used the remaining suds on his own head. After taking turns under the spray, rinsing off, he picked her up, setting her back against the tile. She wrapped her legs around his waist. He pushed into her core, moaning as her body fully accepted him as if they were made only for each other.

Settling into a steady rhythm of thrusts, moans, and gasps, the entire world outside the shower melted away. His crush on Kalani had begun fading the second he saw Nadine for the first time. The horrors of his job seemed distant somehow, like the death and pain of the things he had been a part of no longer touched him while in her arms. You couldn't have the life he led without being affected.

Fear spiked in his gut as the need to feed overwhelmed him. It was so strong it was like fighting the urge to breathe. His mind eased when he remembered despite the ferociousness of his thirst for her, he wouldn't drain her dry. The same intense instinct to feed also controlled when he'd had enough. Nadine shouted his name and a surge of power shot through his veins, coming out the tip of his fangs. The sharp teeth throbbed, demanding her blood. Incapable of denying his body's command, he bit her.

* * *

Nadine

She gasped. His bite stung, and she loved it. Her head spun as her first orgasm claimed her. She floated, although she knew the euphoric sensation was only an experience inside her mind. Withdrawing his fangs, he kissed her.

"Stay with me," he said against her mouth. "When this is over. Stay."

Oh God, she wanted to so badly. But how would a demon and a Bator work? They were supposed to be enemies. She totally didn't feel that way about Riordan. Not with how their bodies fit together, how he offered to save her sister even though he was betraying his kind.

Betraying his kind.

For her.

How could she let him do that? This wasn't supposed to happen. She wasn't supposed to fall for him. She wasn't supposed to lov—

He tilted his head back and roared. His fangs fully extended, sharp, and beautiful. Putting a clamp on her thoughts, she plunged over the other side with him. Again.

* * *

Hours later, they lay in his bed together, fully sated. However, her brain ran in overdrive. She stared at the dresser, debating whether to switch the chains on the pendants. The round pieces of metal looked the same. She couldn't tell them apart, how could they?

CHAPTER THIRTEEN

NADINE

Nadine, Riordan, and Dru assembled in Cutler's office. Kalani barged in moments after the director shut them in together. She ignored Cutler when he growled.

"Whatever, you need me," she said.

"Dru, you wanna address this?" Cutler said.

"She's not going."

Kalani glared at Cutler, avoiding her mate's exasperated eyeroll. He grumbled, and Nadine could guess at what he said in Homodae speak.

"Any*way*...Riory you have the fake?"

"Yep, right here." He patted his chest where the pendant hung from around his neck. A few more specifics were discussed before they all headed out.

"Do you have a way of summoning the Collective?" Riordan asked as the four of them climbed the stairs to the roof. It occurred to Nadine that they may be outnumbered by the demons. But hey, what could go wrong?

"They told me to go to the same place they let me out," Nadine said.

"Would that be Johnson Park then?"

"How did you—never mind, of course you know where the portal is."

Reaching the metal access door to the roof, Cutler pressed his hand to a bio-scanner and the panel swung wide. Night had fallen on the city. Despite the warm breeze that swept through the opening, Nadine shivered. Thanks to Riordan's blood, her wrist was healed and the cast had been taken off.

Riordan put his arm around her shoulders. "Are you cold?"

"Not really."

"You're shaking."

"Wouldn't you be if you were about to face the demons who tortured you?"

"Point taken. We'll be by your side, nothing's going to happen."

God, she wanted to believe him. But with only four of them against an army of bloodthirsty demons, her confidence was low.

"That's right, we'll protect you," Kalani said. "Dawn will here soon and they're not fans." She disappeared through the roof access door.

"She still thinks she's going, doesn't she?" Riordan asked Dru, who trailed behind them on the stairs.

Dru sighed heavily. "Yes, even though I told her she *wasn't.*"

After they were all outside, the door slammed shut. Nadine jumped. Two gargoyles stood sentry at all four corners of the roof, as if guarding over the city in every direction. Storm clouds churned above them, and lightning flashed. A raindrop hit her arm. Then another and another. She put her palm out, catching the light sprinkle.

Riordan wandered to the edge of the roof. Instinctually, she wanted to follow him. However, after her plunge into the laundry bin, she decided to stay in the middle, away from the sides. He vaped onto one of the gargoyles and squatted, his leather pants creaking. His head lurched forward, and he appeared to be concentrating as if he heard something.

God, he's beautiful.

The tremor inside her from when she first drank his blood returned. Pivoting toward her, he smiled, perking up one corner of his mouth and waved her over.

"Uh uh," she mumbled, shaking her head. No way was she getting close to the edge. Even if he was a hottie. And tasted so good. She imagined his thick biceps and roadmap of veins under golden tanned skin...

"What do you mean I'm not going?" Kalani said, cutting through Nadine's thoughts. The Bator female threw her hands up.

Cutler stood opposite her with his hands balled into fists. He puffed his chest as if he anticipated a fight. "We already discussed this. The Collective wants you dead. You're staying behind, and that's an order."

Dru rubbed Kalani's back. "He's right. We can't risk you going."

"That's ridiculous. I'll wear a hat."

"What's that gonna do?" Riordan asked, jumping down from the statue. "Just stay here, we got this. They see you. Smell you even. This exchange turns into an all-out war." When he neared Nadine, the fake pendant bounced on its chain between his pecs under his unzipped hoodie.

Kalani glared at Riordan and growled.

Dru made some of those clicking noises. Nadine wished she knew what he was saying. His mate eventually stopped giving the other two males dirty looks, focusing on him. He purred and kissed her temple.

Envy panged her gut. The couple had something special she may never get the chance to have. Although if the situation was different, she'd like to spend more time with Riordan. But who was she kidding? The Collective wasn't going to simply let her sister go even with the pendant returned. Nadine wasn't naïve. To gain her sister's freedom, she would have to trade places with Penny.

Cutler clapped his hands together. "All right, let's do this." The director's bass-like voice startled Nadine.

Riordan wrapped his arms around her from behind. "Ready?" he whispered in her ear. The warmth of his body gave her a sense of calm. If they could stay like this for a few more minutes...maybe years, that would be lovely.

Nadine refused to answer for fear of letting a sob escape if she opened her mouth.

"Hold tight," he said.

"What if I pass out agaaaaaai..."

* * *

Riordan still had his arms around her when they reformed next to the swing set at Johnson Park. The metal links holding the swings squeaked.

Her head lolled to the side as the dizziness wore off. She pleaded with herself not to pass out again like the first time Riordan vaped them to the Bator Patrol Guard headquarters.

"Take a deep breath," he said. "My blood strengthened you."

"So I won't pass out? Did you read my mind?"

"I can't read your mind, but I can sense your emotions now."

Dru and Cutler emerged out of a swirling mass of black mist. Dru walked about ten feet and raised his hand. "Man, this better go well."

"The voices seem quiet, like there's not that many of them," Riordan said. "Hopefully."

"How do they even know we're here?" Nadine asked. She wasn't sure why she was keeping the lie up. There was no denying the part of her the demons had made her see. She heard them too, whispers in the back of her mind. Ever since the demons fed her blood, white noise crackled in her head. The closer she walked toward the portal, the louder the demons' thoughts became.

"You know we can hear them. It goes both ways," Riordan told her.

I know.

All three males unsheathed daggers. This wasn't what she wanted. Couldn't they have let her come alone? Why did they need weapons for an exchange? If the Collective wanted her, she would go if it meant saving Penny's life.

The sky lightened with the early dawn, however, with the cloud cover, the trees around the park remained in dark silhouette. She couldn't let them get themselves killed over her and her sister.

"I can't let you do this," she said, jumping ahead of them. She faced the Bator Guards with her hands out in front of her.

"Do what?" Cutler asked.

"I can't let you get killed for me or Penny. I'm not what you think."

"Yes, you are," Riordan said.

"No, I'm not."

"Yes." Riordan captured her face in her palms. "I know what you are. I just wasn't sure you did."

Nadine nodded, tears leaking from her eyes. "Why don't you want to kill me?"

"Because it's not your fault." He kissed her forehead, then her lips.

"How long have you known?"

"I suspected all along, but it was the kitty litter thing that completely gave you away."

"Kitty litter. That dirty bastard."

Riordan chuckled. "By the way, remind me that Bastet owes you an apology."

"Who?"

"My cat. Well, she's not mine so much as she claimed me."

"So, Cat is a girl?"

Cutler cleared his throat. "If you two lovebirds don't mind..." The director motioned for them to get moving with a dismissive wave.

Riordan gathered Nadine and pushed her behind him, shielding her with his body. He walked about five feet and then a sucking force pulled them toward the portal, which opened. She counted four figures directly on the other side of the gateway to the Collective. Two of the dark figures came forward but remained on their side of the portal.

Nadine came around Riordan and yanked the pendant from his neck. He held her back. She shoved her closed fist at the demons. "I have what you want. Now give me what I want, and you can have it."

The portal's opening changed from a circle to a tall rectangle resembling a doorway. On either side, Johnson Park seemed to be unaffected by the rip in the Earth's realm. A demon emerged from the

Collective domain. His voice sent shivers through her body as he spoke.

"Hand over the relic." He stretched his hand out, palm up. Although the demon now appeared human, she remembered this one's voice. Not long ago, she'd met him in his true form—a black as tar spiny-backed creature. She recalled how he had sliced her wrists open, allowing her blood to flow until she passed out.

"Not until you let my sister go." Nadine would later replay this exchange over and over inside her head. The demon's words haunted her.

"Hand over the relic." The demon's nostrils flared, his purple eyes blackened. "Or she dies."

"Show her to me and I'll give it to you."

"Nadine!" her sister screamed. Nadine couldn't see her.

"Penny! Where are—"

"Nad—don't give—the relic...pl-please," Penny begged. "I'm already dea—" Abruptly, her voice cut off.

"No!" She shrugged Riordan off, ran around the demon, and through the portal.

CHAPTER FOURTEEN

RIORDAN

Damn, Nadine was stronger now. She'd surprised him by shaking out of his grasp. The demon on their side pivoted. Big mistake. Riordan grabbed him from behind and ripped his dagger across the demon's throat. The demon crumpled to the ground, his body already turning to ash.

Charging through the portal after Nadine,

Riordan expected the entire army to be waiting. Dru and Cutler followed him. The three of them stopped a few feet inside the other realm.

Riordan kneeled. "Are you seeing this?"

"Yeah," Dru and Cutler said.

Riordan had never seen the inside of a Collective realm. A pyramid rose above the horizon, the enormous size dwarfing everything around it. Over the pointed peak hung a red sun. Strangely colored grass was beneath their feet which...moved.

Oh, fuck.

Dozens of black asps slithered around them, rising until their bodies were a foot tall.

Hissssss...hissssss...hissssss....

"Get up, Riory," Cutler said through unmoving lips. "Slowly."

He wasn't sure why he had dropped onto one knee anyway. Awe maybe? Reverence to the Gods? Bator did some strange things sometimes, perhaps on instinct.

"Tell me one of us brought a lighter, matchbook, anything," Dru said.

Briefly, Riordan wondered how Kalani had survived this nightmarish place. He patted the pocket of his hoodie as if some how he'd find a lighter. Why would there be? He didn't smoke.

"No!" Nadine cried out.

Ignoring the possibility of being bitten by the

vipers, Riordan leapt over them, heading toward her. They hissed and snapped at his legs.

Nadine and her sister clung to each other. Or more accurately, Nadine held Penny upright. Something wasn't right. Penny's knees buckled.

"No...no, Penny." Her sister gradually sank to the ground, releasing her grip on Nadine's shoulders.

Catching Penny before she landed on the ground, Riordan swooped her into her arms. Her head lolled to the side. A warm liquid seeped through his fingers. Blood. It came from her back.

"Is she dead?" Nadine asked.

A roar of voices talking in unison bombarded his mind. He closed his eyes and shook his head, trying to remove the invasion. The attempt failed.

Nadine covered her ears.

In a steady cadence, the demons repeated three words: *Prepare for war.*

"We have to go," Riordan said, fighting the mind-numbing chant. And dammit, if he didn't have to carry both Nadine and Penny. "Grab onto my neck, I'll carry you."

Thankfully, Nadine snapped out of her grief for at least a moment and did what he said. She clung to his back with her arms wrapped around him. He wanted to run for the portal but with Penny in his arms, that wasn't an option. The asps parted and slithered into the grass.

Nadine sobbed in his ear, her body vibrating with each breath. "They refused the pendant," she whispered. "Why...why would they do that?"

The other males allowed Riordan and the females first passage into the Earth's realm.

* * *

Nadine

Allowing Riordan's warmth to seep into her, she rested her head on his shoulder. Penny lay limp in his arms. He walked with Penny cautiously, trying not to jostle her too much. Nadine respected the way he took care of her sister.

"I'll take her," Dru said. "So you can vape with your mate."

Mate?

Is that what they thought? She was no one's anything, only a discarded half demon, half human.

Riordan handed Penny to Dru, cradling her head as the exchange was made. Tears soaked Nadine's face. "Be careful with her," Nadine said.

Dru nodded. "We will take good care of her, she will be safe." Although he held her just as Riordan had, the gesture was of little comfort.

Riordan made a soft pumping sound in his throat—not quite a purr, but a sound that eased her mind and sounded unique only to him. Nadine squeezed him tighter and closed her eyes.

Seconds later, they reformed on the Patrol Guard's roof. He waited for Dru to arrive with Penny before heading for the building access door.

"Thank you," she whispered.

"Welcome. I knew you needed to see her before going inside."

The trek down the stairs dragged. She kept looking over her shoulder at Penny in Dru's arms. Where were they going to take her?

Kalani waited at the bottom of the stairwell, propping the door open, her face reserved but compassionate. "I prepared a private room in the clinic so Nadine can be with her for a while," she said quietly.

The private room was so she could say goodbye. *Oh God...*

How was she supposed to do that?

CHAPTER FIFTEEN

NADINE

Dru laid Penny on a hospital bed inside a small room. Behind the head of the bed a soft light turned on. He placed a warm hand on Nadine's shoulder, squeezing gently before walking out of the room.

Riordan came up and stood at her back. She leaned into him. "I'll leave you two alone," he said.

"No. Please, stay." Nadine's voice caught on the last word.

"If you want me to."

She nodded. Taking Penny's hand, she shivered. Her skin was cooler to the touch than when she'd held her in the demon realm, but Nadine didn't let go. Would she ever be able to? Penny had been all she had left of her family. "What will happen to her?"

"That's up to you. We can keep her here until arrangements can be made or—"

"What if I don't want to make arrangements?" A tear slid down her cheek and she sniffled.

"Would you like to have a memorial for her?"

"A *memorial*?" Nadine said, louder than was necessary. "I can't, I—" Her stomach churned.

"I'm sorry, I shouldn't've said that."

Sobbing, she rotated and buried her face in his chest. "It's okay. I know you didn't mean anything by it."

Wrapping his arms around her, he rubbed her back. "Whatever you want to do or however long it takes you to decide is what's going to happen. If that means I move down here and stand guard, I will."

"You would? You'd do that for me?"

"I'd do anything for—"

"You don't have to do anything for me, it's not like I deserve anything."

He took her shoulders and stepped back, looking into her eyes. "Wait, whaaat are you talking about?"

"I killed her."

* * *

Riordan

No way had she killed her sister. Riordan didn't believe it. "What happened?"

"Please don't hate me," Nadine said. "I should've listened to you when you said you didn't want to gamble with her life." She pulled away from him, unable to withstand the way his glowing red-orange eyes searched her face.

"Hmm, you switched the pendants." Riordan glanced at Penny's lifeless body, the dried blood on his hands.

"Do you hate me?"

"Why would I hate you for not giving back the pendant before we figured out what it is and why they want it so badly?"

"I'd feel better if you'd just hate me. Kill me. Tell me what—"

"Stop. I don't hate you, but it sounds like *you* do."

"I killed her." Nadine bawled, taking in shallow breaths, her chin quivering on the exhale. He let her cry because he guessed she needed to let it all out, surround herself with grief until the sorrow was purged. However, this couldn't be done in one day, a week, or maybe even a year.

Nadine took a shuddering breath then went lax. Riordan caught her.

Within a few seconds she opened her eyes and struggled against his embrace. "I killed her!" She flailed her arms. He moved his head out of the way so she wouldn't accidently strike him in the face. "I killed my sister! Lemme go...lemme go!"

The depth of her guilt and shame put a hole in his gut. His heart. His soul cried out as he shared in her pain. "I'm not letting you go."

And I'm not letting you kill yourself.

She wrenched back and forth, still fighting. Then came another shuddering breath.

And another.

"Lemme...go."

"No. Stop this. I'm not letting you go. You didn't kill her, they did."

"I should've given them the real pendant."

"Yeah, and Kalani should have never stolen it. But it's done, now we move forward. We may not like it, but we have to. For Penny. Don't let her death be in vain."

"I just want her back."

"I know you do, but she would've been dead anyway, or at least not living. And here, look." He led her by the hand out of the room and down the hall to Jade's room.

Jade was sitting up, staring at the wall as Kalani brushed her best friend's hair.

"This is Jade," Riordan said.

"Hey," Nadine said, bringing her hand up in a quick half-wave. Jade's blank expression never changed. She merely blinked a couple times. No one knew if Jade heard or understood what was happening. "What's wrong with her?"

"She's catatonic," Kalani said.

"You've heard about this, right?" he asked. "Humans that escape Collectives become catatonic?"

Nadine covered her mouth with her hands. "No. Oh God, I have heard about this. No one has ever recovered. How long has she been like this?"

"Three months with no improvement," he said. "She has it good here, she's cared for at least. Most are stuffed into institutions and forgotten about. So what do you think your sister's fate would be? Sure, Cutler may have allowed Penny to stay with us, but what life would she have? This isn't living."

"He's right, you know. We feed her, bathe her,

she wears a diaper," Kalani said, wiping a tear from under her eye.

"I understand you feel badly, it means you're hu—"

"Part human," Nadine interrupted.

"That's right, but you're better than human. I'm part demon too," Riordan said. "Which means if you hate yourself for that part of you then you must hate me too."

"I don't hate you."

"Positive about that? 'Cuz I gotta say, I'm feeling a little hated over here." Riordan looked at the floor.

"Stop that. Don't *ever* say I hate you." Nadine put her hand on his jaw, bringing his eyes up. "You've only shown me love and respect even when I lied and betrayed your trust."

"I'm a fool."

"You're only a fool because you care about me. I don't deserve you. And I'm afraid."

"Afraid? I don't understand."

"I'm afraid I did those things because it's my nature as a demon. You don't do those things."

"Don't be so sure. We were going to use you to give those bastards a fake pendant, hoping they wouldn't know the difference."

"You didn't though," she said, shaking her head.

"Can I ask you something? What made you

change your mind about the pendant? Why did you switch them?"

"Why did you change your mind about using me?"

"I guess for the same reason you did. We fight our self-serving nature every day. And I dunno, Kalani called me on it."

Besides, life's been better with you in it and I don't want to let you go.

"That's right. You better give me credit," Kalani said. "Seriously, Nadine, I have to check their asses all the time. You don't even know what I go through." She continued mumbling under her breath as Riordan and Nadine left the room.

They wandered down the hallway back to Penny's room. Nadine sat in a chair next to the bed for a long time in silence. Riordan remained in the background, giving her the time she needed with her sister. "Can Penny be kept here until I can make arrangements?"

"We have the facilities, she'll be safe." Taking out his cell, Riordan texted Cutler. A few minutes later two of the medical personnel appeared in the doorway. "It's time. She'll be safe."

Nadine snagged a tissue from the bedside table, wiped her eyes, and blew her nose. Out in the hallway, they walked to the elevators. As they waited for the car, she turned toward him. "Know why I switched the pendants? Because I couldn't let them win. It was also Penny's last words to me, she made me promise and in the end, I didn't want to let her down. 'We fight. We fight until our last breath', and I was like 'where was the Patrol Guard when we were taken?', and she says, 'busy sacrificing themselves for us, even though most humans despise them.'"

"It's funny. I honestly don't care what humans think." Riordan shrugged. "I do it because I enjoy killing them. I mean, think about it. They enjoy picking off humans and we enjoy watching them die. I don't think we are all that different from one another."

Nadine laughed. "There are demons and Homodae that don't like killing."

"I know, I don't think it's for the same reason though. For some of us, it's about the whole service thing. For them it's about leaving their Col—never mind." He smiled sheepishly.

"I'm sorry, how is that any different?"

It's not.

He gathered her in his arms and kissed her. When the elevator arrived, they got on and Riordan pressed the button for his floor.

"Do you think you could love a creature of the night?" she asked as the door slid shut.

"Could you love one with fangs?"

Taking his hand, she said, "I already do. Just promise me that you'll keep me from—"

"Thank you. I *will* keep you." He captured her mouth with a kiss.

She pushed on his chest. "That you'll keep me from doing any more stupid things."

Lacing her fingers in hers, he placed her hand over his heart. "I promise."

Capturing his face in her palms, she drew him down for a kiss. Riordan looked sideways at the 'STOP' button and grinned.

PART THREE

FOREVER
NIGHT

CHAPTER ONE

CUTLER

Some war.

Cutler faced off with four demons. Chaos lay all around him. The small stretch of highway north of downtown Greyfall was littered with abandoned vehicles, overturned police cruisers, and demon ashes. Winds blew the demon remains all over the road, coating everything in a thin charcoal gray powder. The Collective began attacking humans in broad daylight equipped with tinted goggles, protecting their light-sensitive eyes. These raids occurred at random, so the Patrol Guard couldn't properly anticipate them.

How could they defend themselves when they didn't know where or when the strikes would occur?

Being out here all alone wasn't by choice. Thirty feet away lay a fellow Guard. Although the male hadn't moved since taking a blade to his side and left thigh, Cutler sensed Mekhi breathing, albeit shallowly.

Vaporize, dammit.

Anger tore through Cutler and out his mouth in the form of a war cry. He'd left Jade's bedside this morning with a renewed fury toward the Collective for what they did to her. No pain showed on her beautiful face, but something hid beneath the surface.

Snarling, the demons circled him, keeping their feet moving. Cutler stepped forward, moving closer to Mekhi, hoping if he could reach him, he could vape them both to safety. He didn't want to lose another Bator tonight.

What in the hell were they waiting for?

"Come on, bring it!" Cutler had a dagger in each hand. He charged the one barring the path to Mekhi, ripping a blade up the demon's chest and over his throat. Blood spewed from the gaping wound and he hit the asphalt with his knees, his body rapidly turning to ash.

Cutler spun and stabbed another demon in the gut. An arm came around his neck, surprising since he stood taller than these demons. Weakening from his blocked airway, he dropped the daggers. The demon wrenched him to the ground, grinding the side of his face into the asphalt and ash. Luckily for him he couldn't breathe, otherwise he'd have a nose full of the shit.

The remaining upright demon pounced on his back, releasing his throat. Cutler coughed and wheezed, sucking in the ashes. He was flipped over, and the demons spread his arms straight out, palms up.

This. Was. Not. Good.

Vulnerable to anything they wanted to do, he looked up to the sky and prayed. Not for himself, but for Jade and Mekhi. He'd lived many generations, never remembering his old life. He knew about the secret though. Many Bator had asked Cutler why natural births among their species were so revered. The answer, that he never told anyone, was because the babies produced more of them for scientists to re-cultivate upon their deaths. Something from their Egyptian ancestors' DNA allowed this *rebirth*. All it took was a few living cells and a warm fish tank to nurture a Homodae back to life. One stupid bastard wanted them stronger and introduced demon cells to some of the batches.

One of the demons opened a switchblade and sliced Cutler's arm. Blood oozed down the sides of his forearm. What in the fuck? Why didn't they just kill him? He bucked and writhed until the other demon sat on his chest. The heavy weight pushed all the air from his lungs. The demon who sliced him sucked blood from the wound. Ten seconds later the edges of his vision blurred.

"Mekhiiii," he wheezed.

Reaching out with his now free hand, Cutler grabbed a couple of Mekhi's fingers. To vape with another, a connection had to be made. A more substantial hold worked better, but this would have to do; he wasn't leaving the male behind.

With his remaining strength, Cutler willed the vaporization process into action.

* * *

Jade

Jade possessed no sense of time. Nothing seemed real. All she knew was fear, except when he was there. She'd begged him to stay, keep her company. Yet he never listened. He talked though. His words had not made sense, telling her he wasn't giving up on her and she needed to hang on a little longer. Hang on for what? He'd promised to return, kissing her temple.

She sensed a familiar presence except it wasn't him. A woman's voice said her name, continued talking nonsense about the weather being warmer than usual, except all Jade experienced was more cold and dampness like a cave.

CHAPTER TWO

CUTLER

Cutler awoke with a gasp, sitting up in a bed. A moment passed before he realized he was home, safely inside the Bator Patrol Headquarters. Patting his chest, he checked for wounds. On the inside of his right forearm a bandage covered the slice the demon had made there. He ripped off the tape and gauze. Gods, the demon had fed from him.

"Where's Mekhi?" he barked. The door to the room had been left propped open.

Riory stuck his head in. "Alive. Resting."

Although the news was good, he wasn't at all relieved. Now that the Collective had his blood, they would attack. But when? They couldn't exactly evacuate the building with a batch of Bator incubating in the nursery, which meant they had to stay and defend it. Damn. The Collective really wanted the pendant back. Usually, they played a coward's game. This was a bold move for them.

"Riory...Riory!"

"Yes? I'm right outside the door."

"We need to evacuate as many of the civilians as we can."

Confusion washed over the male's features.

"Now!"

Riordan put his palms up. "Okay. What's going on?"

Cutler flashed his arm. "This. Those bastards fed from me."

"Fuck."

Cutler jumped off the bed and grabbed his leather pants from the counter. "Sound the evac alarm," he said, pulling on his pants. An evac meant all non-essential personnel had to leave, but the medical staff attending to the fish tanks stayed behind. Fortunately, the basement level could be sealed off in the case of an attack. They would be safe provided the Guard didn't lose control of the building.

"Let's take a minute to—"

"We don't have a minute. They could be on their way right now."

Riordan gave him a funny look. "Nothing's happened—"

"Why are you arguing with me? I'm giving an order."

"All right, take it easy. Be rational for a minute, what do you want to do about the babies?"

"If anything happens, the lab will have to be sealed. Essential personnel will have to stay here."

"What do you want to do about Penny and Jade?"

"Penny's in the lab's cooler, she'll be fine." But Jade...she couldn't stay in the clinic. Who would look after her? "I'll take care of Jade." Cutler stuffed his feet into his combat boots and headed out. Riordan stood in the doorway, blocking the exit. "Move."

Riordan didn't budge. "Are you sure you're all right? You've been out of it for a couple of days."

Cutler stopped. "What?"

"You didn't know?" Riordan asked incredulously.

"Are you telling me I was out for two days?" Cutler spoke slowly so Riordan heard him clearly.

"Yes, for two days" Riordan chuckled. "Take the

Red," he said, motioning with his head toward the bedside table where three vials sat upright in a rack.

The moment Riordan said 'Red', Cutler's fangs descended. No wonder his arm hadn't healed completely. A second and a half later, the three vials were in his hand with the rubber stoppers off. He swallowed the blood in one gulp.

"By the way, you're right about the evac. I'll go get it started." Riordan left.

He'd lost two days while he took a nap. That was two days of emergency preparations, two days of tactical planning. *Fuuuuck.* Even though two days had passed and they hadn't attacked, didn't mean they weren't planning to. Demons worked at a sloth's pace and weren't exactly calculating, but Cutler started thinking otherwise.

He looked at the facts. The Guard still had the pendant, and Kalani had killed their leader, which meant someone else was in charge. But who...or what?

Out in the hallway, every other overhead fluorescent glowed purple, an indication of an evac in progress. Next door to his room, two Guards shuffled Mekhi out of a room. "Wait," Cutler said. "You good, Mekhi?"

"Getting better, and uh, thanks, for saving—"

"You're welcome." Normally, Cutler would have said something like, *no soldier left behind*, but then there would be an exchange of unnecessary *you-should've-left-me-it-put-you-off-your-feet-for-two-days* and *I'd-never-leave-a-comrade-to-die.* Who had time for all that? Jade needed him. He had idea of how to help her, something he'd contemplated for a while, although was too afraid of disappointment to try.

CHAPTER THREE

CUTLER

How do you love someone you've never met? Well, maybe that was an overstatement. He had met Jade, just never had a conversation with her. This didn't stop him from caring about her, wanting her to wake from the trance so he could tell her how much she'd meant to him. She'd given him purpose other than killing demons.

Cutler carried her upstairs to his room and laid her on the bed. He went over to the flashing purple light by the door, ripped the fixture clean off the wall, and tossed it in the trash can next to the dresser. As if he didn't know there was an evac going on. The building was still safer for Jade than the outside world though. Where would he take her anyway?

Someone knocked on the door. He stood to the side, just in case. "Who is it?"

"Kalani. Do you know where Jade was moved?"

"Yeah, um, check with Bowman," Cutler lied, because if he opened his door and let Kalani inside, she'd be all about protecting Jade herself. He wanted the honors.

"All right, thanks."

Jade stared at the ceiling.

"Hey there," he said, approaching the bed. "Do you mind if we try something?" He waited for her response even though it was silly. "Good. I was hoping you'd agree." Cutler's hands became clammy as he perspired. Was he correct about her? Would feeding her his blood heal her mind like it would her body?

He picked up one of the vials he had drank from in the clinic. He punctured his wrist with one fang, capturing the blood with the glass tube. Cutler had a sliver of reasoning why feeding her his blood might bring her around. Jade never rejected Kalani when she learned her species, and every time he looked at her he experienced déjà vu. Had he known her in one of his past lives? He also reasoned that she was catatonic because she had not had her DNA mixed with demon.

Cutler propped her up, and putting the vial up to her lips, he prayed. "Please work."

He allowed a few drops to coat her lower lip. Giving her food never seemed to be an issue so he wasn't surprised when her tongue slipped between her teeth. She closed her eyes and parted her lips. The eye closing was new. Slowly, he poured the blood, giving her a chance to swallow. After he fed her two more vials, he eased her torso down.

Her eyes remained shut as he set the vial on the table next to the bed. She lay still, breathing evenly. He wasn't sure if she'd fallen asleep. Sometimes she closed her eyes for several hours at a time.

After ten minutes of no change in her, Cutler laid on the bed next to her. He wasn't convinced he was wrong yet, but her recovery didn't seem too likely. Sighing, he ran his hands through his hair.

KNOCK. KNOCK.

"Cutler!" Great, Kalani was back at the door.

"What?"

"I checked with Bowman and he said he saw you take—"

"Yeah, I know, I've got Jade in here." Fortunately, he'd remembered to lock the door, so no one could get in using the bio-scanner. The box chirped its *access denied* warning.

"What are you doing in there?"

"She's fine. I'll look after her."

"Can I see her?" Kalani's impatience came through in her tone.

"She's staying in here and she's sleeping."

"We should probably get her out of here."

"Where do think she'll be safer? She's better off with me."

Kalani growled but he caught her meaning. Knowing she wouldn't go away without seeing her best friend first, Cutler scooted off the bed and opened the door. She peeked around the door jamb. "Oh, she is sleeping."

"What did you think, I was lying?"

"You're acting strangely, and you've been out of it for a couple of days."

"I'm fine. Trust me, I won't let anything happen to her."

Kalani smiled lopsidedly. "I do believe that. I see how you care for her. Just, if you need anything, I'm—you know, I think you'd really like her if things were...different."

"If she weren't catatonic, you mean."

Kalani nodded. "Yeah."

Cutler closed the door. Jade remained unmoving with her eyes closed. He sat on the end of the bed, hanging his head low.

* * *

Jade

A shaft of light shone into the cave through a small hole. For the first time since she could remember, Jade made out the shape of her hands. Crawling toward the light, she reached out. The voice that comforted her grew louder, his words making little sense. Not exactly true, she understood the words, but didn't know how they pertained to her in the context of this cave.

He spoke of feeding her blood, hoping for a cure. A cure to what? She wasn't sick, she was trapped. She moved closer to the light source. Chunks of blackness broke away, creating a larger opening. If only she could get to the hole...

A bigger section of the cave crumbled. Yes. She scrambled for the opening, his voice growing louder...

CHAPTER FOUR

CUTLER

Sometime in the early morning, Cutler awoke out of a deep sleep. The exhausted kind where you thought you were only out five minutes. He groaned and rolled his to side.

Shiiiit!

Jade was gone. The side of the bed she had lain was cold.

He yanked open the drawer in his side table and grabbed the pendant, the real one, and put it on over his head. Leaping to his feet, he ran for the door, flinging the metal panel into the wall so hard the lever door handle bent. Thank the gods he'd fed her some of his blood or he'd be a raging lunatic right now.

Cutler vaped outside Riordan's apartment. The purple lights above his head had stopped flashing. The evac was complete. He didn't bother knocking on the door, he used his override instead.

Nadine yelped when the door hit the wall. Riordan roared, putting a protective arm over her.

"She gone!" Cutler yelled. "Get up!"

"Who? Oh, fuck! Jade? *How*?"

"Fed her my blood."

"That's never worked bef—"

"She's Bator minus the demon."

Riordan's forehead crinkled. "Is there such a thing?"

"Yeah. There is."

"Since when?"

"Since always. Get dressed, I need your help. I take it there have been no signs of demons around the building...in it?"

"No, but the scouts are on the roof and across the street. Anything suspicious and we'll know about it."

They had his blood. Why weren't they attacking? Lulling them into a false sense of security? Cutler stepped out into the hallway, giving the couple privacy while they dressed. "Meet me up top," he called to Riordan.

Four minutes later, Cutler paced along the edge of the roof. Riordan came through the access door. "Took you long enough."

"What? Five minutes," he said. "Have you been able to sense her?"

"No," Cutler snapped.

"All right, maybe she went home. Kalani gave the address, it's in Jade's file."

Cutler knocked on his head. "I got it. Let's check there first." So stupid, he should have locked his door from the inside too, so she couldn't get out. One thing he was certain of, Jade wasn't in the building. Gods, if something happened to her...

* * *

Jade

Jade crawled toward the widening hole in the cave wall. Dark turned into light. When she emerged from her prison, she found herself in a dimly lit room. She nearly screamed at the man lying next to her in a strange bed. A flat screen hung from the wall above a dresser and light shone into the space from a cracked doorway. She slid her feet onto the floor, glancing over her shoulder, hoping she wouldn't wake the man.

Not wanting to be shut inside another darkened place, she fled the room. She padded down a hallway with bare feet. Her clothes consisted of hospital scrubs and a diaper. Dammit, she had to ditch this thing before she went any further. She found a door marked 'STAIRS' and tried the door handle.

Locked.

A box with a glass front and palm outline stuck out from the wall next to the door. With no reason to suspect her handprint would unlock the stairwell door, she pressed her hand to the palm reader. A thin green bar of light passed up and down under her hand. The beam made several passes. By the third scan, her impatience grew. "Please work."

A tiny light on the door turned from red to green and the lock clicked.

CHAPTER FIVE

JADE

Jade squeezed through the iron gate surrounding her family's estate under the padlock and thick chain. The gate and the security alarm sign on the front lawn were the only things protecting the house from demon attacks. However, the attacks usually took place on the highway like it was a sport to them. She couldn't remember the last time someone's home had been targeted.

A lone flickering light shone through a window on the second floor, likely a fire burning in the fireplace. The air didn't seem warm enough for summer. A breeze kicked up, ruffling her hair and spreading goosebumps over her skin. How much time had she lost in her dark prison?

Her eyes itched and burned. She rubbed them. Must be the cooler air.

Even though she wanted to run inside the house screaming she was home, Jade crept toward the front porch steps. The alarm sign was bent over, lying almost flat on the grass. She studied it a moment. Perhaps the lawn people ran it over with their mowers, except the grass looked like it hadn't been cut in weeks. What the hell? Her father would have made them fix the sign, he always inspected the lawn after each cutting—something he done since he'd retired and had no one to boss around.

The bushes next to the porch rustled. Gasping, her hand went to her chest. Two birds squawked and flew away. She walked up the steps. The door was shut, but where the deadbolt should be was a hole. Crouching, she peeked through the void in the door. Darkness stared back at her.

She would have turned away at this point if not for the nagging pull inside her chest. She rubbed her sternum over her heart in circles. Pushing her way inside, Jade kept low. Fortunately, she knew her way around the giant house in the dark for when she used to sneak out as a teenager. Long gone were those days. She missed the false sense of protection the estate offered. No one had really been safe though.

Jade made her way across the foyer and climbed the staircase. She began counting the twenty-seven steps, holding the railing next to the wall. ...*three...four...five...si—*

"Ow, shit." She landed on one knee, hitting the riser. Her hand on the balustrade kept her from face-planting. She patted the carpet, wondering what she'd tripped on. Unable to identify the object in the dark, she cringed at the possibilities. The thing was cold and wet.

Oh, God.

With her eyes burning again she moved on, tripping two more times. At the top she glanced left and right. The left was toward the room with the fireplace and beyond that her former bedroom. The pulling insider her screamed louder. Her hands curled into fists and she squeezed her eyes shut. She couldn't resist the compulsion to move forward. What the hell was this? Never in her life had she felt this strongly about anything. Despite everything in her mind telling her to leave, she inched along the wall, deeper into the hallway.

The door with the fireplace had been left open. She peered around the doorjamb. The sofa faced the fire. Orange glowing light silhouetted a head. Her breath hitched. She pulled her head back and flattened to the wall.

Who is that?

Where were her parents?

At the end of the hallway, shining blue beams of light glowed from under the bottom of her bedroom door. Her heart raced, every beat pounding hard. She ducked past the doorway to the study, knocking her hand on the frame. Jade bolted for her bedroom, forgetting about the stranger in the house. She flung open her door, crossing her arms over eyes to the blinding light. "Stop it!" she yelled. Why on Earth had she done that? Nothing made sense, she didn't even know what she was doing. Why had she come here instead of her apartment?

The light dimmed. On top of her bedside table sat a statue of the Egyptian goddess Isis. The fainter blue glow emanated from a disk embossed with a winged scarab wedged in the space between the goddess's hips. Jade's obsession with Isis and the ancient culture probably led to her never fearing Bator. She was thrilled to learn of Kalani's secret, but kept her feelings hidden. Her grandmother had given the statue to her as a present when she was ten.

She moved toward her bedside table then picked up Isis. Using her fingernail, she pried at the edge of the metal disk.

Her eyes watered. For no reason at all, she knew she needed this disk. This was why she came here. "Come on," she begged. As if on command, the thing popped free of its mounting, along with a chain connected to the back. For a moment, she wondered if anything was real—that she was still trapped, only had moved onto a bigger nightmare. What happened to her parents? Who was the stranger in their house?

The stranger.

There was a slow hiss behind her. She whipped around. In the doorway, blocking her only way out, stood a man. No, a creature like the ones she saw inside the Collective. Although not completely tar-colored, it did have a hunching back and clawed hands. Another hiss, then the demon charged her.

Jade screamed. The demon roared, eating the distance between them in long strides. Its purple eyes narrowing their focus to what was in her hand.

The disk heated. Light shot out both sides of her fist. She raised her arm, letting the pendant drop from her middle finger by the chain. "No!"

The demon didn't slow.

"Stop!" she commanded.

Nothing changed, the demon still ran toward her.

"Blind him!" A brilliant light blasted from the pendant. She clamped her eyes shut as the room lit up.

There was a thud, followed by a moan. She opened her eyes. The creature lay at her feet, writhing on the floor.

* * *

Cutler

Cutler ran around Jade's apartment, checking all the rooms, opening closet doors. "Jade! Jad—"

"She's not here," Riordan said.

"Where the fuck is she?"

"There's the possibility she—"

"Don't you dare finish that sentence. Don't. Fucking. Do. It." Cutler refused to even acknowledge that Jade could have been taken by demons again. Unless he had definitive proof, no way would he believe it. His fangs descended.

Taking a deep breath, Cutler tried sensing her presence. If she were relatively close by he'd know it. Shit. He couldn't focus. Telling himself to relax wasn't much help. His mind was creating all sorts of worst case scenarios that included her being ripped apart by a gang of demons.

"I *was* going to say maybe she went to see her parents," Riordan said.

"Please tell me you know where they live."

CHAPTER SIX

CUTLER

"Looks like someone shot out the lock." Riordan pointed out the obvious. Although, in the male's defense, Cutler had been thinking it.

Unsheathing a dagger, Cutler pushed open the door, the hinges creaking. He sensed his blood in Jade somewhere in the surrounding area. The buzz grew more intense the closer they came toward the mansion.

Riordan followed him inside, also with a dagger in hand. Man, there were so many times Cutler had wished a bullet would kill one of those bastards. Nope, only a slice to the neck wouldn't heal, like their own Achilles' Heel. Wrong mythology, but a fitting comparison. He scoffed at the word 'mythology.' If humans only knew. Hell, if the other Bator knew the full truth.

Lab-bred, my ass.

Cutler stepped on something that crunched. Nocturnal vision was fantastic but also created a whiteout effect, making objects appear less detailed. He glanced at the floor. From the shape he determined it was shards of broken tile. "Careful. The floor's busted up," he said to Riordan.

"I saw that."

"Could've have warned me."

"You're leading the way, aren't you?"

"Shhh." Cutler put his arm up, signaling him to halt. His muscles tensed.

Jade.

They were getting closer or she was heading toward them.

At the top of a grand staircase, Jade appeared. She ran down the stairs, glancing over her shoulder. Debris dotted the steps, trash mostly, and smashed pieces of what might have been furniture at one point. And...bodies, well parts of bodies. He counted too many arms for it to have been only one.

When Jade hit the middle of staircase, her foot caught. She pitched forward, flying over a few steps. She screamed.

"No!" Cutler shouted, instantly vaporizing. His arms reformed, grabbing her out of the air. His mist billowed, swallowing her.

They both reformed outside on the front porch steps and he hugged her tightly to his chest. She struggled against him. He took her biceps and held her away from him. She kicked his shin and screamed. Cutler grunted. "Jade, stop. We aren't going to hurt you."

Kicking him again, likely for scaring her, she ended her tirade. She kept her head down. "You can put me down now."

What? Oh, shit, he had her raised off the floor about a foot. "Sorry, I'm Cutler," he said, setting her on the ground. "The male in the house is Rior—" A necklace with a circle pendant dangled from her hand. The chain and the size of the thing looking exactly like the one around his neck.

There are two?

Riordan came outside. "What was chasing you?"

She looked up for the first time. Her eyes, which had been green yesterday, burned red-orange like his. Although her pupils weren't as pointed and feline-like either, they had begun stretching top to bottom. Cutler's pride swelled knowing his blood had started the process.

"We can't stay here, as much as I enjoy watching you two make eyes are each other," Riordan said.

"I woke up next to you," she said.

"Yes. I should've stayed awake, been there for you."

"You're him."

"Him?"

She nodded. "Your voice...I heard your voice. Inside that place."

"What place?"

"I dunno. I remember getting out of the Collective. Kalani rescued me. Then, I dunno, I was trapped someplace."

"Can you describe it?"

"It was dark and cold. Damp like a cave."

"You couldn't see anything?"

"No." She shook her head. "It was dark."

With a trembling hand, she tucked her mahogany hair behind her ear.

"Uh, we gotta go. Can't you discuss this later?" Riordan shifted his weight from foot to foot. "She was running from something, right?"

"Shut it," Cutler barked.

"Demon, and I blinded him," she said.

"Uh, usually there are more," Riordan said.

"There's not."

"And how do you kno—"

"Do you sense any? If you're so concerned then do a sweep of the house," Cutler said. Riordan threw his hands up and backed off. "How did you blind him?"

"With this," Jade said, holding up the necklace. The pendant twisted and finally settled so he could see the design on the face. "Oh, it stopped glowing."

Cutler held the piece in his hand. "A scarab. Hmmm." He pulled the pendant around his neck out of his t-shirt and showed her. Both necklaces glowed.

CHAPTER SEVEN

JADE

The glowing pendants pulled toward each other like magnets. The necklace around Cutler's neck forced him forward, and the one Jade held slipped from her grip.

The pendants fused together, shooting bright blue rays of light in all directions. A shockwave blasted all three of them off the porch. Jade landed in the evergreen bushes next to the house. Cutler lay on his back on the lawn about twenty feet away with the fused pendants on his chest, only a dull light emitting from them. Riordan sat up rubbing the back of his head just off the porch on the walkway, seemingly dazed.

Jade ran to Cutler and checked for a pulse. "I don't think he's breathing." The other male who she didn't catch the name of hurried over and kneeled next to him. "What do we do?" she asked.

A second later, he ran a blade across his wrist. Dropping the dagger, he shoved his arm under Cutler's neck, tilting his head back, forcing open his mouth. Blood dripped into Cutler's mouth. Jade had heard blood smelled like pennies in large quantities but never before had she understood that. And this was hardly a large amount, yet the scent overwhelmed her. However, instead of getting sick, she wondered what it tasted like.

At first Cutler didn't respond, then he swallowed the blood. The male put his wrist closer to his lips, and eventually Cutler's Adam's Apple moved up and down faster as he drank.

After a few minutes, he pushed the arm away and tried sitting up.

"Whoa, lay back a minute."

"What happened? Why do I feel like someone threw me into a wall?" He wiped blood off his lower lip. "Is this yours?" Cutler asked the male whose name she didn't know.

"You died."

"So you fed me your blood?"

The male shook his head and looked at her. "I'm Riordan by the way," he said.

"Hi. Your voice sounds familiar."

Riordan smiled. "Really? I read to you when you were...um..."

"Out of it?"

"I was going to say catatonic. But yeah, that works."

Jeez. Her cheeks warmed. Embarrassing much? She had a diaper on when she awoke. Jade retreated into herself for a moment. "Do you know what happened to my parents?"

"Do they have another house somewhere?" Riordan asked.

"You don't think they were killed by demons, do you?"

"Did your parents have people who tended to the house? Maids or anything?"

"Yes, but only a couple. Oh God." She swallowed hard. "They're all dead."

"I'm so sorry. There have been an increasing number of daytime attacks all over the city."

"Why is this happening? Is this because Kalani rescued me?" She wasn't sure why exactly she thought she was so special that a war would start because of her. Tears stung her eyes as she thought of how her parents may have died. Had her mother been taken to the demon realm to be used as a blood bag? And if she had, how long realistically would she survive?

Cutler stayed silent. Riordan's expressed grew tight.

"She should have left me to—"

"To die? No, don't say that. This isn't your fault," Cutler said.

As Jade sobbed, Riordan put an arm around her shoulders. "I'm sorry. We can have someone go in and collect your parents."

"You mean their bodies? I wanna see them." She shrugged his arm off her shoulders and ran for the porch.

"You don't want to do that." Cutler appeared in front of her, wisps of black smoke swirling around him. She ran into him, unable to stop her forward momentum. He caught her by the elbows.

She wanted to punch him. "Why not?"

"Because it's not safe and...*gods.*"

"Get out of my way!" She beat on his chest with her fists, but he remained in the same spot. Steady. Unmovable.

"I'm sorry for your loss," he whispered. "But I can't let you go inside."

Why not? she wanted to scream. Except she knew the answer. Her mind tried blocking out what she knew as the truth. The thing she had tripped on was...oh God, a body part? Yes, it was. Later, she would thank Cutler for protecting her.

The blind demon staggered out of the house, falling down the steps. He landed on his back. Black holes filled the place where his eyes had been. Riordan came over and sliced the creature's throat. The body turned to ash, losing its form and crumbling into dust.

What are those blades made of?

She wondered if the metal had special properties or that was just what happened to demons after death. Swiping under her eyes, she straightened up, sucked back her tears. "Can you get me out of here? I'd really like to see Kalani, if I could."

"She's at headquarters," Cutler said, examining the joined pendants.

"Can I see those?" Jade asked. Her hands shook with anticipation. He took the chain off his neck and handed them over. Cradling the necklace with her trembling hands, she flipped the two-sided pendant from the scarab side to the crook and flail. Jade stared at the thing, mesmerized by the intricate details. The glow brightened. She couldn't look away, rapt by a vision that carried her to another place and time. Images of a once truce between demons and Bator. Cutler, or a male resembling him, stood alongside a black spiny creature like the demons she saw inside the Collective realm. Each were given a pendant, but the demon betrayed the Bator, killing him, and stealing his necklace. A battle began, and the Bator retrieved one of the pendants before fleeing to the safety of Earth's realm. Bitter warfare had waged ever since.

When she looked up, both males had concerned expressions on their faces. "What?"

"Where did you go?" Cutler asked. "We've been calling your name for ten minutes."

Did I disappear?

"Collective realm."

"You went catatonic. We thought we lost you, again."

"Uh uh. I'm fine," she said, putting on the two-chained necklace. "We have to go."

Chapter Eight

CUTLER

It didn't take a genius to figure out Jade knew something she wasn't telling them. The three of them vaped to the Patrol Guard rooftop. She rubbed her eyes then squeezed them open and shut.

"What's wrong?" Cutler asked.

"My eyes have been stinging and itchy since I woke up."

He nodded.

"Why are you nodding? They hurt."

"I wanna show you something. It might explain things." He led her down to the stairs and to his apartment.

"What do want to show me?" she asked as they went inside.

"Look in the mirror." He ushered her into the bathroom.

She gripped the edge of the counter, shoving her face closer to the mirror. "What the *hell*? My eyes changed color?"

"Yes. But more than their color changed."

"Huh?" She pulled down her right lower eyelid in the mirror. "Freaky. I look like a cat."

"I take it you didn't know what you are?"

She faced him. "No. I mean, yes. I dunno. I've felt different from everyone else. My nana was the only one I ever was truly connected to."

"It's possible she was Bator. How old were you when she died?"

"Just after my eleventh birthday. The year before that she gave me a statue of Isis, I thought because she knew of my obsession with Egyptian stuff. She told me to keep it safe. That's where I got the pendant. It was stuck in it."

"How did you know where it was?"

She studied his face, but he gave nothing away.

"As soon as I woke up, a force I couldn't explain or resist drew me to it." Confusion washed over her face. "How did you wake me up or did I do that?"

"I gave you blood."

"Yours?"

"Yes."

"Did I like it?"

"You drank it, so I suppose."

"I've never had it before."

"Exactly what I'm thinking."

Cutler's favorite cat wove herself through his legs, purring. Femi liked hiding under his bed. She surprised him because of her shy nature. "Well, I hope you like them."

"What, cats?"

"Yep." Bending down, he scooped her off the floor and cuddled her.

"Aw, she's pretty—it's a girl, right?"

"Yes. Her name's Femi. She must like you, because she's usually hiding under the bed."

Jade stroked her black fur while Femi purred.

"I must say, you're taking this 'you're a Bator' news well."

She shrugged. "Well, I always wanted to be one. Is that weird?"

"No. But you're asking the wrong person."

"Have you ever wanted to be an ordinary human?"

"Gods, no. What would make you ask that?"

"I dunno, humans fear you...us. Wow, that sounds strange."

Cutler smiled, his fangs making an appearance. "Do you think I'll grow a set of those?" She touched a finger to her eyeteeth.

"Possibly. I really don't know, but your eyes changed, and I didn't know that would happen."

"What made you try giving me blood?"

"Last ditch attempt. Nothing else worked. We took you for walks, showing you pretty much the entire building, talked to you—"

"You talked to me every day. I couldn't see you, but I could hear you. It was comforting and I would envision what you looked like, which helped get me through."

"How did you picture me?" Femi squirmed and jumped onto the counter. She sat at the edge of the sink, licking her paw then wiping her head.

"You said you showed me around, so I must've been able to walk, and I assume my eyes were open?"

He nodded.

"You look like what I thought. Well, mostly. I knew you were Bator. Same square jaw, fangs, dark hair. Handsome."

"You think I'm handsome? Did you hear that, Femi? She thinks I'm handsome."

The cat meowed.

"I think she agrees," Jade said, giggling.

"Hello?" Kalani poked her head in the bathroom. "Remember me?"

Gods, why didn't I lock the door?

"Lani!" Jade threw her arms around her best friend. They held each other for a long time. Cutler scooted out of the tiny bathroom into his bedroom to give them some privacy. After a few minutes they left his apartment laughing like girls did, as if he weren't even there. Jade didn't say goodbye or 'thanks for waking me.' He was forgotten, traded up for a better model. He couldn't blame Jade, it wasn't if they really knew each other. Despite this fact, breathing became a little more difficult.

CHAPTER NINE

CUTLER

Cutler stood at the edge of the roof, scanning the city street below. The tiny cars zipping up the street and around the blocks looked like matchbox cars from this height.

"Things have been too quiet tonight," Mekhi said from behind him.

"Hey, glad to see you back on your feet. I was wondering if you'd come back."

Mekhi smirked and shrugged. "You know I can't stay away from this place. Besides, something's brewing and if you think I'd miss that action because I got a little boo boo, no way."

"Respect."

Mekhi gave him a stiff nod and went to relieve a guard on the other side of the building.

Damn. Was this attack even going to happen? It had been four days since those demons drank his blood. "What the hell are you waiting for?" he said. He never told anyone what happened with the pendants, and as far as he knew neither did Riordan. Kalani may know now though.

Going back inside, Cutler made his way to his apartment. Femi was lying on the bed. "How's my girl?"

Meow.

After giving her a quick scratch behind the ears, he hopped in the shower. Ten minutes later he laid on the bed under the blanket. The Patrol Guard were given the option of gray or navy bedding. He went with the dark blue. Gray was just so drab.

Cutler glanced at the clock on the bedside table. *3:02 AM.* And he was wide awake. He hadn't seen Jade around since she took off with Kalani yesterday. Some of the civilian staff had been coming to work during the day. It had been ingrained in them to avoid the dark, except they didn't seem to get that they were in danger during the day now. But whatever.

There was a knock at his door. Since no alarms shrilled or flashed, he ignored it, rolled over, putting a pillow over his head. "Go away."

The lock on his door released. Would he never learn to lock the door from the inside? "Cutler?"

Jade.

He quickly rolled back over. But shit, he was naked.

"Can I come in?"

"If you want."

"You don't sound too convincing. I'll come back another—"

"No. Come in." *I'm only naked.* "I want you...to."

She stepped inside and closed the door behind her. Jade had changed her clothes and she smelled delicious. He licked his lips. He never been this attracted to anyone before. And what was he saying? She didn't know him. He didn't know her either, even though he'd sat with her every day for three months. Just because he wanted her didn't mean she wanted him. He let his upper body flop back.

The mattress depressed as she sat on the end of the bed. She rearranged her position so she faced him. "Sorry I left without saying anything yesterday."

Holding a hand up, he said, "You don't need to apologize. I get it."

"What do you get?"

That you don't want me. "She's your best friend." *I don't rate.*

"Yeah, she is, but you rescued me."

"That was all her, I—"

"Not the way I see it." Jade's chest glowed blue under her white dress.

"Why does it do that?"

"I dunno, it seems to react to my emotions sometimes." She took a deep breath. "I have to tell you something." Jade kneeled on the bed and scooted closer to him. Gods, he was so naked. She placed her hand on his thigh.

His entire body tensed, blood rushed south. "What is it?" he eked out when she hesitated. She removed her hand and his whole body screamed in protest. He clutched the sheet.

"I know what these pendants are for. I haven't told Kalani, and actually she doesn't even know I'm wearing them. I don't think she knows."

"Knows w-what?" he breathed. To his own ears he sounded in pain.

"Are you all right?"

"Yes. Knows," he gasped when she put her hand on his thigh again, "what?"

Again, she took away her hand.

His body sagged. That was until she started rubbing his thigh. Again. "Do you like this?" she asked.

"Please...stop," he whispered.

"I don't think you want me to."

"What I want is irrelevant. Tell me what Kalani doesn't know."

"Why it is irrelevant?"

"Because you don't want me like I want you."

"Oh, you're a mind reader?"

"No. But I don't think you know how naked I am under this blanket."

"How much more naked can you be than naked?"

He snort-chuckled. "Tell me what Kalani doesn't know, please."

"That Bator are reincarnated. I saw you in the vision I had when I held the joined pendants the first time. I'd say based on how the people were dressed, what I saw took place thousands of years ago."

"I know."

"You do?"

"I mean, I don't remember it, but I know of our true history. All directors are told so someone can preserve our history. Demon DNA was introduced this century."

"I'm adopted. My parents never told me..."

"Your grandmother."

"Yes. She told me then gave me the Isis statue."

"There's something the human world doesn't know. The Bator Patrol isn't run by the government like people believe. We offer our services in exchange for money and the right to be left alone. We exist *because* they leave us alone."

"Whose idea was it to introduce demon DNA to the mix?"

"Mine." Cutler laughed. "Well, not exactly me, but my former self, who clearly was an idiot."

"There are humans working here."

"Everyone needs a job."

* * *

Jade

Jade stayed on her knees. She and Cutler looked at each other, letting the silence hang between them. Who was her grandmother? Could it be that the pendant's energy brought them together? Jade was certain her nana wasn't Bator. Maybe with the reincarnation thing some memories stayed in the

DNA. No matter the reason, she could stop the war. Permanently.

"A lot to take in at once, huh?"

"Yeah. But you know, I'm okay with it." She'd finally found her purpose and knew what she had to do, but would she have the courage to follow through?

"Good." He smiled, showing off his fangs.

Jade ran her tongue over her front teeth. Yep, still blunt. She pushed on her cheeks where her sinuses had starting throbbed this morning on and off. "Hmmm," she moaned.

He gave her a look of concern. "You okay?"

"I think I might be getting a cold or something, my sinuses ache."

Cutler put his arm behind his head. "I might have some cold medicine in the bathroom. You're welcome to it, if there is any."

"Thanks. But I think it'll be okay. I'm not sneezing and my nose isn't dripping." She really didn't feel sick and hated taking medicine except for an occasional aspirin. Over-the-counter stuff made her lightheaded. She sighed heavily, and not because she was bored or tired. She had been down in Kalani and Dru's apartment awake on the roll-out bed they brought in, so she wouldn't be alone. She went over her in mind what she discovered in the vision. Bator had the ability to reincarnate. Cutler had been her mate but was killed in a battle over the pendants. She saw the events unfold as if she was experiencing it for herself. She'd caught her reflection in his eyes. The vision gave her something else too—all the memories of the life they shared thousands of years ago. Nope. Uh uh. More than that. She lived the life with him all over again. To Cutler and Riordan, she never left the lawn. Yet to her, a lifetime had passed.

Jade needed to tell him the other reason she came to see him and wouldn't leave unless he asked. At this point, he'd have to drag her away in chains. When he had introduced her to Femi, she almost choked on her spit. They lived with a cat he'd named Femi.

"Listen, it's late and Kalani's probably sent out a search party for you by now," he said.

"How come you're kicking me out?" She gave him her best pouty expression, however, she wasn't faking.

"I have to go to the bathroom."

"You know your bathroom has a door, right?"

"I know, but I'm naked."

"I've seen you naked before."

His head snapped in her direction. "When did this happen?" He chuckled. "Why wasn't I made aware of this?"

"You're on a need to know basis."

"You're serious."

"I told you I saw you in my vision."

"Yeah," he said, coughing. "But you didn't say I was naked."

"Not the whole time."

He scrubbed his face with his hands. "All right, I'll bite. But hold that thought, I was serious about needing to use the bathroom." Cutler edged off the bed in a such a way she only saw his behind. What a spectacular ass.

"Go ahead. Can't promise I won't peek though." He glanced over his shoulder, grinning. She stopped breathing. The expression on his face had been one she'd seen a million times. If she didn't tell him how she felt now, she may lose her nerve. "Make love to me." Oh, Gods, had she just said that? It wasn't exactly a declaration of love, but what else could she say?

You don't know this yet, but I love you and feel like I've waited thousands of years for your return.

She'd sound nuts.

"Ah, um..."

Shit.

"Forget it, that was stupid. I shouldn't—"

"No, no, don't forget it. I'm—yeah, surprised is all. Can I use the bathroom first?"

"Please." Jade made herself comfortable while he tended his business. She tried out different positions on the bed, thought about being nude when he got back...

When he returned to the room, he hadn't wrapped a towel around his waist or anything. His fangs were fully extended, his hard, muscled body the work of an art master. Finely crafted just the way she loved.

"You're peeking," he said.

"So are you," she said, glancing down.

"Not yet."

A wave of heady heat washed over her body, settling at the apex of her thighs. In her mind, they were already making love.

He came up to the bed. Getting on her knees, she met him at the edge.

Reaching down, he grabbed the hem of the dress Kalani had loaned her. She raised her arms over her head and he lifted it off. He took her face in his hands but didn't kiss her right away.

"So are you going to tell me why I was naked in your vision?"

"Maybe." *I want to tell you everything.* She remembered every touch, every joy, and every sorrow they shared together. A tear slid down her cheek.

He captured the droplet with a kiss. "Why are you crying?" he said, softly.

"You died in my arms."

"Is that why I was naked?"

She pushed on his chest. "No. What's wrong with you?"

He chuckled. "I'm kidding, I'm kidding. I was trying to lighten the mood. I don't want you crying *before* I make love to you. You can cry after, but not before. Well, no, that's not true. I don't want you crying ever, especially, if I was the one who hurt you."

Gods, he still had the same sense of humor. He also knew how to make it impossible for her to stay mad at him.

"You'll have to tell me more about this vision. First I was naked then I died."

"You were not *naked* when you died, all right?"

Cutler smirked. "Why was I naked then?"

"If I have to explain it to you—"

He cut her off with a kiss. "How 'bout you show me instead?"

"Lay down and I will."

Straddling his hips, she rested her hands on his chest. He cupped her breasts then smoothed one hand around the back of her neck, bringing her down for a kiss. As they made love, she pondered, for a moment, the idea of soul mates. Jade had never understood the term until now.

CHAPTER TEN

JADE

Jade smiled at Cutler lying next to her. They had spent all day together in bed, alternating between bouts of sleep and sex.

"Oh, shit, Jade, you're bleeding," Cutler said, sitting upright.

"Where—oh, my mouth." What new hell was this? She covered her lips and rushed into the bathroom. He followed her and stood behind her at the sink. Without checking the mirror first, she splashed water on her mouth until the water ran clear again.

He grabbed a towel. "Let me see."

Lifting her eyes and head to her reflection, she opened her mouth. *Oh, my gods...*

Fangs. She had fangs!

She turned around and hugged Cutler. The pressure in her cheeks hadn't been because she was getting a cold. She was growing fangs.

"Congratulations, they're beautiful."

"I know, right? Wait until I show Kalani. She was already so excited about my eyes." Jade looked into the mirror again. "My eyes too, they're full slits."

"Beautiful." Cutler kissed her.

Going back into the bedroom, she looked under the bed for Femi. "Look, sweet girl, fangs!" The cat crawled out and meowed.

Cutler laughed, but it wasn't at her, he laughed because he shared her joy. "She's happy for you." Tears rimmed his bottom eyelids. "You wanna test those beauties out?"

"Yes. I totally want to bite you." Leaping into his arms, she wrapped her legs around his hips. She struck the vein on the side of his neck hard and fast.

* * *

Cutler

After her feeding, they settled into bed. He had no intention of leaving the room again. Ever. Okay, that wasn't going to happen. Reality would find a way to ruin a good time.

"Hey, you never asked me what the pendants are for," she said, lying across his chest.

"That's your secret. As I said before, I don't think it's a mistake they wound up in your hands."

Jade lifted her head from his chest. "Yeah, but why do you say that?"

He stoked her back in lazy circles. "I don't have the answers, but they found you for a reason and obviously they hold a power only you seem to be able to control. Think about what your vision is trying to tell you."

"I'm not sure I like what it's telling—"

A shrilling noise blared, followed by a robotic voice. *"Warning. Security breach. Warning. Security breach. Warning…"*

Yep. Reality. Ruined. All.

Without having to say anything, Jade got dressed too. She held the pendants in her closed fist around her neck. Cutler armed himself and they left the apartment. Peering around the doorjamb, he first made sure the hallway wasn't under attack.

The warning alarm grew louder as they stepped out into the corridor.

"Will someone turn that thing off?" Cutler groaned. Several guards ran in front of them, down the perpendicular hallway. "Let's go," he said, taking Jade's hand.

"Hey, don't worry about me, I have my protection."

Although he hadn't personally witnessed her blinding the demon at her parents' house, he had no doubt the power of the relic she possessed.

They rounded the corner in the direction the guards went. A few cats scrambled through cat doors, hissing and growling. But one cat sat at the end of the hallway by the stairwell access. Bastet. That cat had claimed Riordan as hers. "Did he go this way?" Cutler asked Bastet. "Up the stairs?"

She flicked her tail up.

"Thanks." Cutler slammed his palm on the bioscanner, releasing the lock on the door.

BOOM!

"That didn't sound good," he said. Chunks of cement fell down the shaft and a cold draft swept through the stairwell. He looked up but couldn't see what had caused the loud boom. "Do you think you can vaporize?"

"Is there a trick?" Jade asked.

"Not really. You will it, if that makes any sense."

She looked at him like he had horns on his head. "I'm not sure how to *will* something."

"Clear your mind of nothing but getting from one place to another. I dunno, nobody taught me, I just did it. Think about the top of the stairs, I guess."

Jade closed her eyes, and she must have held her breath because her face turned red.

"It's not necessary to close your—"

"Shhhh, I'm trying to concentrate."

"We don't have time for this, you can try again later. Like when we are not under attack." He wrapped his arms around her and willed them to the top of the stairwell.

Wind blew through a gaping hole where the door had been. Cutler pulled Jade to the side of the gap. Sticking his head around the corner, he counted the number of demons on the roof.

Fuck me.

He saw at least ten, and three Bator. The demons were still half in their natural state, spines protruding from their backs, clawed hands.

Metal scraped leather as he unsheathed his daggers. He held one out to Jade.

"I don't know how to use that."

"Take it anyway."

She shook her head. "Uh uh. I won't use it."

"You will if you need to. Trust me."

"I do. You need to trust me too."

Cutler took a deep breath, exhaling slowly. She'd shredded his heart. "Stay here." Preparing for battle, he vaped through the ravaged doorway.

CHAPTER ELEVEN

JADE

Stay here.

That was probably a great idea, considering she had zero fighting skills. Cutler disappeared, leaving behind a wisp of black smoke. How bad could this battle get? Demons couldn't vape. How many could be on the roof? She stepped into the doorway.

Annnnd, she got her answer when

phosphorescent blood sprayed her in the face and a demon hit the ground at her feet.

"Get back!" Riordan roared.

Jade yelped, jumped back, and dove into the stairwell landing—banging her knees and elbows. Holy shit! She counted how many demons...a dozen maybe? And too few Bator. More demons were climbing over the side of the building onto the roof.

BOOM! BOOM! BOOM!

The metal grated landing she lay on vibrated. She put her head down, covering the back. The *booming* grew louder and the vibrating increased, making her body bounce. Gods, she hoped the sound wasn't more demons stomping up the stairs. But if it was Bator, wouldn't they vape?

No. No, no, no.

She sat up and pushed herself into the corner. Clutching the pendant, she tried like hell to become invisible. It wasn't happening though.

Black smoke swirled in front of her. She tucked her feet closer to her body. Once the guard fully formed, he headed down the stairs. "Stay put."

Someone screamed two levels below her. A large object or something she imagined was substantial in size thudded against the stairs, sending tremors up through her body.

BOOM! BOOM! BOOM!

The demons still advanced despite the screaming

and thuds. Demons outnumbered Bator. This was no big secret. How had they avoided a planned attack before? For thousands of years? Through her vision as detailed and real as it was, Jade never discovered the answer.

She looked at her hand holding the fused pendants. Yes, she understood what power they possessed together. However, power of this magnitude required someone pure of heart with an untainted soul to wield. Was this her? She knew the answer. Jade had lived her life with humility. Although wealthy, her parents gave to charity whenever someone asked, and even when they hadn't. Kind to everyone, for the sake of kindness, not because they wanted anything in return. Gods, she loved them. Her chin quivered. They hadn't deserved their fate. Hating demons was a natural reaction and she wasn't above this notion. But committing genocide for revenge? She couldn't.

Apart, the pendants held only small bursts of energy. Together, they could destroy an entire species. What she only guessed was the truth had been buried to protect everyone. The problem with this logic, demons knew the secret and would do anything to keep the pendants apart.

How was she supposed to stop a war without annihilation?

Her head pounded.

Think, Jade, think!

BOOM! BOOM!

Four demons made it to the top of the stairs and rushed her. Kalani appeared, shielding her from an attack. "I'll kill you all," she growled.

BANG! Guns sounded louder indoors. Outside, a 9mm made a pop noise. She knew about guns from going shooting with her uncle against her father's protests. Her best friend dropped. Jade screamed.

"No, you bastards!" Jade had leapt to her feet so quickly, she wasn't aware of moving. Then she caught the black smoke twirling around her body. Her fangs descended and sounds she'd never heard come out of her mouth before rose from her chest. Oddly enough, the series of noises made sense.

"Bow before me or tonight will be your last," she said. Understanding seemed to register in their expressions and body language. At least, they halted their advance for a moment.

Kalani grabbed her ankle with a bloody hand. "Jade," she whispered. "W-What are—"

"Stay down, Lani."

The demons didn't bow.

Dammit, don't make me use this.

"Stop!" she spat, holding the pendant out from her chest. The disk glowed brightly, forcing the demons to cover their eyes. Reaching down, she touched Kalani. "Hold onto something." Jade counted on the wall to catch her. The pendant jangled, beams of blue light shot in every direction. She turned her head. This was going to hurt but everyone's survival was in jeopardy. The chains burned her hand as the pendant turned bright orange, glowing like piece of hot coal.

"Brace yourselves!" she roared.

The atmosphere warped as the relic sucked the air around them toward it. He hair blew forward. Demons scrambled for something to hold onto. However, she remained standing, unaffected by the gale force winds. Her hand glowed where she held the chains. She wasn't going to let go no matter how painful.

The winds intensified. "Hold on!" she screamed.

Jade had only one choice.

Destroy the relic.

The metal disk shrank until only a marble-sized light hung in the air by the chains. Light exploded outward. Then came the shockwave, knocking everyone over and sending the demons on the landing tumbling down the stairs. The last thing she remembered was hitting the cinderblock wall.

Chapter Twelve

JADE

A white light shined in one of her eyes then the other. "Jade, can you hear me?"

"Ahhh." Really? She snapped her jaws at the unsuspecting doctor, but darn it, missing his hand. The human stepped away and Cutler stood over her.

"How're you feeling?"

"Alive." She sat up. "I might to ask you the same

thing." Bruises covered his face and he sported a split lip.

"I'm fine, nothing blood won't cure."

"Thank gods. How's Kalani?" Jade swung her feet over the side of the clinic bed.

"Whoa. She's fine. Lay back down for a minute."

Jade sighed heavily.

"What exactly did you do to the demons?" Riordan asked, leaning against the doorframe.

Cutler glanced at him then at her again. "Yeah, *what* did you do?"

"Nothing," she smirked. "I didn't do anything."

"Well, they all fled," Cutler said.

"They didn't say goodbye either. I'm heartbroken. I really thought we could be friends too," Riordan said. Nadine, whom Kalani had introduced her to, sidled up to him, wrapping her arms around his waist. He kissed her temple.

"Yeah, I think some even left skid marks," Cutler said.

Nadine left her mate's side and approached the bed. "Is this okay?" she asked.

"Yes."

"And is this okay?" Without warning, Nadine embraced Jade. "Thank you. I can't thank you enough. I'll thank you for the rest of my days."

Cutler raised an eyebrow. "Wha...?"

"What?" Jade shrugged.

Nadine said, "Can't a girl be grateful?"

"I guess. We're all grateful, but what exactly is she grateful for?" Cutler asked.

Okay, okay, so she had made two choices. After all, demons killed her parents.

"I thought I'd have to live like that forever. I never realized how much noise they made inside my head." Nadine smiled.

"Oh," Cutler said.

"Now you get it, huh?" Jade said. "I severed their connective link to one another. Permanently. No more hive mind mentality. I knew they relied on it and also made them stronger, because it also linked their energy, and collective energy is stronger energy. The pendants showed me that."

"You're welcome," Kalani said. Dru rolled her in the room in a wheelchair. She wore a sling on her right arm.

"Lani!" Jade got off the bed and hugged her best friend.

"And what are we supposed to be thanking *you* for?" Riordan asked.

"For stealing the necklace from their leader. You're welcome."

Everyone laughed. Jade supposed she was correct.

Later that night, Cutler and Jade lay in their

bed, their bodies sated and intertwined. "I couldn't destroy them," she said.

"I know, and I'm glad you didn't."

"You are?"

"Why do you sound surprised?"

"Oh, I dunno. They've been our enemy for thousands of years."

"And they will be for thousands more. Committing genocide is not the answer. You could never live with yourself and I couldn't *live* with you, if you had."

"So you're not mad at me for saving them?"

He chuckled. "Have I given you any indication that I'm angry? Hell no, I'm not mad, I love you, and apparently have for thousands of years even though I didn't know it."

"I love you too."

He kissed the back of her hand. "I have one question though. Why was I naked?"

Jade giggled. "Here, let me show you."

***Thank you for reading The Gods of
Greyfall Collection!***

If you enjoyed this book please...

Share your copy with a friend who might enjoy it.

Consider leaving a review on Goodreads, Amazon,
or other retailers that carry the book. This lets other
readers know if they might enjoy reading it too.

Find out about my other books by visiting my website:

ajnorrisauthor.com

ACKNOWLEDGMENTS

Many heartfelt thanks to...

My family, friends, and readers for their continued support. I couldn't do this without you.

Lydia Harbaugh for putting up with my ramblings and angst. You are the best!

Felicia A. Sullivan for being amazing.

A special thanks to Mary Margolis for naming Riordan and contest winner, Heather Cuva for naming Jade.

ABOUT THE AUTHOR

A.J. Norris is a romantic suspense and dark paranormal romance author. She enjoys being able to get inside someone else's head, even a fictional one, and see what they see. Watching how her characters deal with difficult situations or squirm with the uncomfortable ones makes the hard work of writing all worth it.

A.J. loves going to the movies, watching her son play baseball, and communing with other writers. She's a member of two writer's groups and RWA. She lives in southeastern Michigan with her family, who are extremely tolerant (at least most of the time) of all her late nights behind the computer.

Sign up for A.J. Norris' newsletter for updates and exclusive content at https://www.ajnorrisauthor. com/a-j-norris-newsletter-sign-up

ajnorrisauthor.com

www.ingramcontent.com/pod-product-compliance
Lightning Source LLC
Chambersburg PA
CBHW020245200626
46816CB00001BA/141